FORTUNE'S FALLEN

FORTUNE CHRONICLES 1.5

KATHLEEN MCCLURE

PUBLISHED BY OUTRAGEOUS FICTION

Fortune's Fallen Copyright © 2019 by Kathleen McClure*

***This Work was originally published under the title *The Longest Shard*.**

Cover by Youness Elh
Edited by Claudette Cruz

ISBN: 978-1-947842-28-1

Thank you for choosing *Fortune's Fallen*.

If you enjoy the journey, please consider leaving an honest review. For individual creators like me, your feedback is the best way to help other fans of quirky science fantasy discover our worlds.

And for more outrageous fiction, including new stories, exclusive content, and reader community, scan the QR code below to follow our Outrageous Crew on Ream. It's free, easy, and the best way to delve into our fantastical worlds!

Happy reading,

Kathleen

https://reamstories.com/outrageouscrew

ABOUT THE FORTUNE CHRONICLES

The Fortune Chronicles are a series of standalone adventures featuring a colorful cast of characters who wander through each other's narratives from time to time.

We hope you enjoy your visit to the distant future and the planet Fortune, where tech is low, tensions high, and heroes unlikely.

For Dr. Deborah King, for helping us all through the Barrens.

Success is as dangerous as failure.
Hope is as hollow as fear.

— LAO TZU

CHAPTER 1
BACK IN THE DAY

Fort Echo - Northern Adian Territories
December 3, 1441 After Landing

Gideon blinked sleet from his eyes and turned to the woman to his right. He had to squint because Sergeant Nbo Mulowa was upwind, and looking in her direction meant facing the sideways-falling mix of ice and rain.

"Why didn't you say so before we struck camp?" he asked, pitching his voice to pierce the rain and wind currently pounding the plains they were slogging across.

"I did say so," Nbo protested from under the hood of her stolen Adian cloak. All he could see of his sergeant was the puff of her breath as she added a bitter, "Repeatedly."

"As did I," the man to Gideon's left pointed out, bringing Gideon's gaze over to where Lieutenant Eitan Fehr skimmed the handheld torch over the slick ground.

Normally, Gideon would have nixed the light, but for

tonight's prize he'd chosen a different or, as Nbo put it, *suicidal*, approach.

"It's not that crazy a plan," he said to both his doubting subordinates. "Anyway, if it turns out we can't steal the 'ship, we'll still be able to blow it up."

"You mean, like we were ordered to do?" Nbo asked, shaking the sides of her cloak so an extra flurry of drops joined those falling from the sky.

"I believe there was some leeway in the operational specs," Gideon offered, turning back in the direction of Fort Echo, which he and his company had been watching for the past two days from the height of a nearby plateau.

During those two days, Gideon and his company had observed a number of supply caravans enter the fort from the south and east roads. Once inside the camp, the fort's troops steadily moved the cargo from their mech lorries and crawlers into the hold of the ARAS *Bounty*.

An apt designation for a supply 'ship, one Gideon believed was being readied for a journey to the Allianzan front, where a host of Adian legions were wintering.

On reporting these suspicions to Epsilon Base, Gideon was pleased to hear his superiors agreed with his assessment that the *Bounty* must not, under any circumstances, deliver those supplies to the Coalition forces.

But while the brass back in Epsilon believed the best way to prevent such an occurrence was for Gideon and his company to destroy the airship, Gideon looked on the *Bounty* as honey in the comb for the Colonial Corps.

Gideon hated to waste a good comb of honey.

So he'd come up with his own plan, one that would deprive the Coalition of their winter stores, not by destroying them, but by appropriating them for Colonial use.

"The brass might even agree with that assessment," Nbo offered now, "if you had ever flown an airship."

"Fehr has." Gideon waved in the lieutenant's direction.

"A few short training flights, in good weather," Fehr qualified. "But I've never landed an airship."

"I've seen enough landings to get us to anchor," Gideon assured him. "Plus Hamish was a flight engineer before he joined the infantry, so he'll have engine pods covered, right, Ham?" he called over his shoulder, to where Specialist Hamish Costanza led the small column of infantry.

"Right as rain, Colonel," Hamish replied, his waving hand flapping out of his stolen cloak. "Learned all there was to learn about these Adian rattletraps from my auntie."

"Your auntie's a Coal-fart?" Corpsman Walsingham asked.

"No such thing." Hamish sniffed at Walsie's suggestion. "But she was a right scavenger, was Auntie Megs, and you'd be amazed what all finds its way into the rehab yards."

"See?" Gideon said, turning back to Nbo. "Ham's got us covered."

"I admire your optimism, sir," Nbo said, in the tone Gideon knew meant *You're a few bees shy of a hive.*

"It'll be fine," he said. "And if my plan goes swarm, we've got the crystal det on hand to do the needful."

"As long as we don't do the needful at eighteen thousand meters," she muttered.

Gideon opted to ignore that, and turned to continue their trek to the camp's southern gate, the closest to the fort's airfield. "Almost there," he said, then glanced at Nbo. "Join the company, Sergeant. And Hamish?"

"Sir?"

"Stop singing."

"Was I singing?"

"Yes, Hamish," Gideon said, sharing an eye roll with Nbo

before she fell back to join the specialist who had returned to a froggy rendition of his favorite Earth ditty about taking a break from all your worries.

As Hamish's concert subsided, Gideon and Eitan stepped up to Fort Echo's southern gate, where a humanlike shadow separated itself from the gatehouse.

"Who goes there?" the shadow demanded over the drumming precipitation.

CHAPTER 2

DAY 1

Morton Barrens
Maximum Security Penitentiary
February 9 1442 After Landing

"Let me be as clear as the crystal you will soon be harvesting," Warden Simkins intoned from the balcony atop the prison's outer wall, "this is not some risto-friendly rehab camp."

"Well, smog it, I want a refund," Manny, the convict to Gideon's left, whispered.

His comment earned a chuckle from the convict to Gideon's right.

The nearest corrections officer shifted, but said nothing.

"This is a working prison." The warden let his eyes skim over the five newcomers while the suns glinted off the deep umber of his shaved head. "And it is through your labor that you will make restitution to the society you have wronged. You will also learn, and quickly," Simkins added, "that these walls are not your prison."

"Could'a fooled me," Manny muttered.

"The suns are your prison," Simkins boomed. "The demands of your own bodies are your prison. And should any of you decide to test your luck—to walk away from your work party, or climb the walls of the yard in an attempt to escape— you have my promise that no one will stop you. But in so doing, you will be consigning your bones to the suns. I will waste none of my officers on seeking wayward inmates, just as I will punish no inmate who changes their mind and chooses to return."

He allowed that to sink in before adding, "But if you do take the walk, and have a change of heart, you must turn back before reaching your 9,562nd step."

"That is an oddly specific number," Manny observed as Simkins stepped back and the corrections officers began herding the newest inmates through the prison's main gate.

Less than an hour later, Gideon exited another gate, dressed in the dull gray uniform worn by all Morton inmates.

His clothes and personal belongings were gone, locked away in a small box by a stone-faced corrections officer.

Everything.

Including his coat.

To Gideon, losing the long-coat of the Colonial Infantry was akin to losing a limb.

Who was he, if not a soldier?

An idiot, Dani would say.

Thinking of Dani, his hands clenched, then loosened again, as the motion caused a fresh stinging.

He glanced down at the 66987 that another stone-faced guard had just tattooed on the back of his hand.

Feeling more than a little stony himself, Gideon turned from the mark of his crimes to scan the yard into which he'd spilled.

The square of gritty soil was larger than he expected, and

dotted with the occasional bench or slab of rock, which he saw some inmates making use of to read, or play a game of cards.

One convict, a nonbinary named Cher who Gideon recalled from the airship, was sitting on one of the stones, in a way that put Gideon in mind of a civilian he'd once seen in the aftermath of a pitched battle waged on the streets of Macintosh. The man had been sitting just so—hands clutched, eyes empty—on the stoop of a burned-out building, while company after company marched past, on their way to the next engagement.

Shaking off the memory, Gideon turned from Cher to study the walls of the enclosure. Three of them, including the one from which he'd just emerged, were formed by the two wings of the cell blocks, each two stories high. The third, he'd been told, held the mess, the infirmary, and the administration offices.

The fourth and final side of the yard was defined by a wall Gideon figured a determined double amputee could climb, if they really wanted.

But as the warden had pointed out earlier, the only time an inmate would want to climb that wall would be if that inmate were feeling suicidal.

The wall, and the roofs of the buildings, were topped by parapets along which the corrections officers walked, their crossbows loaded with rubber-tipped riot bolts. But, Gideon noted, each of the guards also carried quivers of live bolts at their hip, alongside thick club-like sticks he knew to be crystal-powered shock batons.

"How's the hand?"

"*Keepers.*" Gideon spun to face another inmate.

"Sorry," the man said with the whisper of a smile that matched his genteel Avonian accent. "Didn't mean to startle you. I'm Doc," he added, by way of introduction.

"Gideon," Gideon replied automatically as he eyed the

man. Lean, graying, and observing Gideon through a pair of spectacles. "Is that a nickname or a profession?"

The eyes behind the spectacles crinkled while the whisper of a smile became more of a statement. "Both, as it happens. Which means it's me who'll be stitching you up should the need arise." The smile twisted a bit as he added, "The staff physician prefers to stay on the staff side of the wall."

"Ahh," Gideon said as another inmate emerged from one of the two cell blocks.

"Hey, Doc!" the new guy, another Avonian, called out, his deep brown eyes shining with a pleasure that was completely out of place, given the kid's current location.

Gideon wondered what kind of pharmaceuticals Doc might be handing out to the general population.

"Hello," he greeted Gideon. "You must have just got in. I met Manny already. He's in his cell and looked kinda down."

"That's natural, under the circumstances," Doc pointed out.

"Sure, excepting that I also spied Renny walking away from Manny's cell right before I got there."

"Ah," Doc said.

"You should watch out for Renny," the kid said, turning to Gideon. "He's a scary son of a sabertooth, and no mistake. Even scarier than Pavel."

"Pavel?" Gideon echoed the name. He was starting to feel dizzy.

"Context, Nyal," Doc murmured. "Pavel Escamilla," he continued to explain. "In for person-slaughter, assault and battery, willful destruction of property and . . . well, the list goes on. Mostly because Pavel keeps adding years to his sentence every time he thinks another inmate looked at him funny."

"Good to know," Gideon said, determining that, at no time, would he be looking at anyone, ever.

"But at least Pavel is predictable," Nyal said. "Renny's just mean."

"Like a bully on the queen pitch mean?" Gideon asked before he could stop himself.

"Like hiding a dead tarantula under Kneecaps Mololo's pillow because she scored the last portion of tea at breakfast mean," Doc explained.

"I don't think Kneecaps has slept a night through since then," Nyal offered.

Gideon thought it would take a lot to unnerve someone who went by the name Kneecaps.

"Not to give you the wrong idea," Nyal said, as if suddenly realizing the dire picture he and Doc were painting. "Generally everyone here gets on pretty well."

"Uh-huh," Gideon said.

"No, but truly," Nyal said, his brown eyes brimming with sincerity. "Even after a day in the veins, someone's almost always ready for a game of cricket or net the queen or basketball. And Doc's mad for his card games."

"True enough," Doc agreed.

"And sometimes Lonnie puts together a show," Nyal continued. "He's in for counterfeiting, but his real love is theatre. He even used one of my models, a replica of the Hollywood Bole, in a shadow play about Yggdrasil. And once we even—"

Gideon held up a hand. "I appreciate the sales pitch," he said, "but I'm not looking to join the local knitting circle here."

"Good thing, since the warden won't let us have any needles," Nyal said thoughtfully. "But you might want to get into the Go tournament. We call it the Go-on-Forever tournament, because, well, look where we are. And Pavel sponsors centipede races, because he's got a collection of them."

"You and Pavel have fun with that," Gideon said, "but I

think I'll just skip the self-delusion portion of my incarceration, if it's all the same to you."

"Oh." Nyal blinked and seemed to shrink into himself. "Well." His shoulders slumped and he shoved his hands in his pockets before walking away, with a great deal less energy than he'd arrived.

"That was unkind," Doc observed.

"You think it's better for him to live in some fantasy?"

"What I think is that Nyal exemplifies the power of the mind over adversity," Doc replied.

"Sounds like a load of cog-wash," was Gideon's opinion. But he glanced over to the youth, now crouched near one of the walls. He appeared to be folding a scrap of paper into a draco. "What's a kid like that doing in a place like this, anyway?"

"He may look young, but Nyal is of age," Doc said. "Just as he was of age the night he blew a safe in a bank he thought to be deserted." Doc glanced over at Nyal's hunched shadow. "When he found the remains of the guards inside, he walked out of that bank, away from the rest of his crew, and up to the nearest copper to turn himself in." He glanced back at Gideon. "Unlike you, Nyal believes he belongs here."

"What makes you think I don't belong here?" Gideon asked evenly.

"I didn't say that," Doc pointed out. "I simply observed you *believe* you don't." Then he, too, walked away.

"Always good to see a fellow soldier in this muck heap."

Gideon's lip twisted as he turned to see yet *another* inmate coming to a halt at his side. "Are you a sensitive?" he asked, eying the dark-haired, suns-burned stranger.

One ink-black brow arched. "Hardly."

"So what makes you think I'm military?" Gideon asked, even as his self reminded him, vigorously, he wasn't in the mood for another conversation.

"The way you stand," the man replied, as if it were obvious. "The way you scanned your surroundings, and the enemy," he nodded at the guards pacing the walls above, "the second you stepped into the yard. Then there's the way your hand moved towards a weapon you're not carrying when you heard my voice."

Gideon glanced down, saw his hand was, in fact, resting where his shooter would have been holstered, if he'd been wearing it. "Points for being observant," he said. "Bet that's helped you acclimate, since you've only been here, what, two . . . maybe three . . . weeks?"

The dark eyes narrowed at that. "And what makes you think I've been here such a short time?"

"Your skin's more burned than tanned, which tells me you haven't had time to adjust to the desert suns," Gideon said with a shrug. "Also, your uniform hasn't started to fade, and it's still holding the creases from the original folds. Your boots are dusty, but not broken in, and your hand is still inflamed from the tattoo."

"Well played," the stranger said, flicking a glance at the reddened flesh around the numbers etched onto the back of his hand. "I did, in fact, arrive in this charming little facility two weeks and three days ago. Renny Boucher," he introduced himself with a crooked tip of the head.

"Gideon—"

"Quinn, yes. I know," Renny said. "Word travels," he explained. "And what did you think of the warden's welcome speech?"

"I'd say he had a shot at the Hollywood Dionysus prize," Gideon said, once he caught up with the whiplash change in topic, "but the judges would have to shave off a few points for the scenery chewing."

"On the contrary," Renny said, "I wager they'd give him higher marks, as there's so little scenery in the Barrens to chew."

Gideon almost laughed, which was a strange sensation, given the circumstances.

Circumstances including not only where he was, or why, but also that, from his accent, Renny Boucher was almost certainly from Adia—one of the Coalition states against which Gideon had, until very recently, fought.

"And now you're thinking how I'm not from your native Colonies," Renny said.

"Are you *sure* you're not a sensitive?" Gideon asked.

Renny dismissed that with a flick of his hand. "The curse of being the lone Adian in a Colonial prison."

"And how did you manage to become the lone Adian in a Colonial prison?"

"That would be a long story."

"It's not like I'm going anywhere," Gideon said, unable to entirely mask the bitterness of that truth.

"No urge to take a long walk, then?" Renny asked, inclining his head towards the joke of a wall.

Gideon followed his glance and recalled Simkins's dire warnings. "Not just yet."

"Good." Renny fixed his oddly intense gaze on Gideon as he added, "All in all, I'd prefer to be the one who ends you."

"Excuse me?" Gideon asked.

"No," Renny replied, and as he did, the unnamed intensity in his eyes resolved itself into a bone-deep hatred before he walked away, leaving Gideon gaping in his wake.

CHAPTER 3
DAY 6

Gideon's first week of harvesting was spent in an isolated tributary of crystal that curved around a spit of sandstone, just out of sight of the parent vein.

All the newcomers were given remote sections. The reason being, if an inexperienced harvester were to detonate a cluster of the silicate, the rest of the party and—more importantly—the larger vein would be spared.

Whatever the reason, Gideon was fine with the removed location.

Here, there was at least a measure of privacy.

Every once in a while a CO would wander by to assure themselves he was still there, and working, but beyond that, his only company was the occasional scarab or lizard scrabbling over the rocky spit, and the constant hum of living crystal.

For Gideon, it came off as more a pressure behind the ears than an actual sound. From what he'd heard from the other prisoners, however, there were a few convicts who ended up going swarm from the ceaseless not-quite-a-sound.

Since most of those so driven were also rumored to be sensitives, Gideon figured he was safe, given he was about as sensitive as the bed of shard he was currently trying to loosen.

Shard had been another jump on Gideon's geological learning curve, because it wasn't until he was forced to harvest the stuff that he learned crystal only ever grew from shard. And shard, he also soon discovered, was smogging hard. Hard enough that one could only get the crystal out of the ground by taking the shard with it.

It was a long, painstaking process, but Gideon found he didn't mind the labor.

Partly because any form of action was better than staring at the wall of his cell, or the dust in the yard, or the dried food pellets served in the mess, all of which allowed far too much space for thinking.

All in all, better to be out in the veins, shifting grit, wrestling with shard and taking great care not to jar, rattle, or otherwise disturb the delicate crystal growing from said shard.

"Well, look here. If it ain't Himself, all alone inna veins."

Gideon looked over his shoulder. "Hello, Lonnie," he greeted the bearish figure.

Lonnie's first love might, as Nyal claimed, be the theatre, but his current appearance indicated he'd decided to moonlight in the "How to Make Gideon's Life Hell" society.

"I hear you were Corps before you came to the Barrens." Pavel Escamilla—the same Pavel Gideon had been warned of—appeared at Lonnie's side, bristling with animosity.

"Was," he said to the Stolichnayan giant, turning to scoop out another pile of dirt. "Now I'm just another number . . . like you."

"Not like us." A voice which Gideon recognized as belonging to Mama Callas, a Fordian out of Moosehead, joined the party. "We may be criminals, eh, but we ain't no traitors," Mama continued.

As her voice ground through the air like the gravel he was moving, Gideon wondered why the COs were allowing so many prisoners to wander into his work site.

Probably because most of the COs hate your guts, his self informed him.

Since many of the COs were ex-military, Gideon supposed this to be true.

He glanced Mama's way. "I hear you're in for smuggling a shipment of this stuff," he said, nodding towards the sparkling river of crystal.

"Yeah." She frowned, her brows furrowing as she glared at the silicate. "What about it?"

"Word has it you lifted the shipment from a Corps resupply lorry." Gideon paused, stretched, heard his back crack, then looked at her again. "Stealing weapons' grade crystal from the Corps during a time of war strikes me as more than a little treasonous."

At which point a laugh, followed by Renny, slid around the spar of rock. "He does make a point," Renny said to Mama, while throwing Gideon a smile that would look at home on a crocodile.

"Renny," Gideon said, as if greeting an old friend over tea. "What's the buzz?"

"Nothing yet," Renny said. "But in a few minutes, everyone will be talking about how my friends and I—"

"Ain't your friends," Mama interrupted him.

"Only here because you're paying us," Lonnie agreed.

"And I like hitting people," Pavel added.

"My *temporary employees* and I," Renny corrected, "are going to be breaking a few of your bones. Maybe even your jaw."

"That sounds bad," Gideon decided before returning his attention to the small mountain of dirt he'd built up through the morning's work. "Lucky for me," he said, "you and your employees won't be doing that."

"Oh? And why ever would we not?" Renny asked, while the other three inmates shifted to block Gideon from any escape.

"Because," Gideon said, driving his spade into the pile of discarded earth, "I happen to be holding the Spade of Hesitation."

At that, Mama let out a snort. "And what on toxic Earth is the Spade of Hesita—"

She never got to finish the sentence, as the spadeful of dirt hit her in the face.

Mama got off easy, however, as Pavel got the *actual* spade upside his head.

While Mama spluttered and tried to clear her eyes, and Pavel dropped like a felled tree, Gideon shoved the butt of the spade into Lonnie's prodigious gut, then swept the head around to drive Renny—who was now holding a long, oily black dagger Gideon realized was made of shard—a few steps back.

From that point on the fight got muddy, but because Gideon never stopped moving, and kept a firm grip on his spade, he was able to hold on to the advantage.

Or he did until a whistle shrieked across the desert and a handful of corrections officers finally arrived, skidding to a halt in a cloud of red dust.

Gideon watched them take in the scene.

From their expressions, they'd been expecting to see Gideon bleeding out in the veins.

He could only imagine their disappointment in finding him standing—mostly untouched—with his spade held in front of him like a quarterstaff, while the remaining inmates sat, lay, or staggered blindly through the vein.

"Drop the shovel and get on the ground," CO Menk growled at Gideon.

"Actually, it's a spade," Gideon said, but he did as he was ordered, dropping flat on the ground, hands behind his head, while the other guards swarmed over the remaining combatants.

"You always thought yourself clever."

Gideon angled his head to the right to see Renny . . . also flat out, and spitting blood into the dirt.

There was no sign of the dagger, but Gideon felt certain Renny had stowed it safely out of the guards' view.

"How would you know?" Gideon hissed the question.

Renny merely curled his lip as Mama said, to no one in particular, "I still don't get it. What's the smogging Spade of Hesitation?"

CHAPTER 4
DAY 22

Gideon limped his way out of the motor pool with the rest of his work party, the aches of a long day in the veins exacerbated by the bumpy ride to and from the work site in the prison crawler.

Morton's staff mechanics, as Gideon soon discovered, didn't worry overmuch about the comfort of the prisoners. Their efforts were largely focused on the reinforced crawlers responsible for carrying the day's harvests to the prison warehouse.

Which made a certain amount of sense, considering a bruised inmate or two might be cranky, but an un-planned crystal detonation would ruin pretty much everyone's day.

So Gideon accepted the aches of the day as best as he could and, as he entered the tunnel leading to the yard, thought longingly of a cold beer, a hot meal, and a solid fourteen hours' rack time.

Since this was the Morton Barrens, he was resigned to a tepid liter of water—some tea, if he was lucky—a bowl of nutrition pellets, and maybe seven hours of sleep.

As those seven hours wouldn't even begin for another four,

he decided to find himself a piece of empty shade, where he could at least enjoy the sensation of not moving.

A nice idea, and one that was quickly squashed as the flow of bodies around him ground to a halt, stalling his shade-ward progress.

The weary mumbles that had accompanied the trek from the motor pool rose in frequency, becoming murmurs of anticipation.

Curious despite himself, Gideon worked his way past Pavel's shoulders to see a handful of inmates who weren't on the work party—including Doc—standing next to a pair of over-stuffed satchels.

As he watched, everyone in the yard, no matter how tired, immediately congregated around those satchels.

"Mail call," a voice near Gideon said, and he turned to see Renny at his side.

He'd heard nothing and seen little of the Adian inmate since the attack at the vein. "Not expecting any letters?" he asked as Renny made no move to join the throng.

"Alas, my subscription to the *Domino Times* was not forwarded to the Colonies."

"Okay."

"How about you?" Renny asked, easing to one side as a pair of inmates, heads bent over a newspaper that had to have been a month old, almost walked into him. "Expecting any correspondence?"

Gideon spared him a glance. "No."

"In that case . . ." Renny held his arm out, allowing Gideon to spy the gleam of his shard peeking from under his right sleeve. "We have unfinished business."

Gideon thought again of a place in the shade. "What are the chances you'll hold off on this until my muscles have had a chance to recover?"

Renny's free hand rose, rocked from side to side.

"Didn't think so," Gideon said. "Well, let's get this over—"

"Quinn!" Doc's voice preceded his appearance. "Gideon." Doc offered Renny the briefest of nods before holding out an envelope. "You've received a letter."

Gideon took the offered piece of mail automatically, though he couldn't think of anyone on Fortune who'd be writing to him.

Then he looked at the flowing script forming the address . . . and knew.

He didn't need to see the return post, but he flipped the envelope over anyway, and wasn't surprised by the clutch it caused in his heart when he saw her name.

Lieutenant Indani Solis
Second Jump Unit
CAS Phalanx
ACPO Epsilon Base

"Pretty name," Renny commented, reading over Gideon's shoulder.

Gideon held the letter out to Doc. "Send it back."

"Are you certain?" Doc asked.

"Are you insane?" Renny demanded at the same time.

"Yes," Gideon said to Doc. Renny, he ignored.

"If you don't want to read it now . . ." Doc began.

"I will!" Renny said.

"It's not addressed to you," Doc pointed out.

"I can pretend it was."

"No one is reading it," Gideon snapped at Renny, then turned to Doc. "Send it back," he said again, still holding the envelope out.

Doc sighed, but accepted the letter. "I'll put it in the outgoing mails."

Gideon nodded his thanks. As Doc moved on to find the next mail recipient, Gideon turned to see Renny still at his side. "Still want to dance?"

"Maybe tomorrow," Renny said, still studying Gideon. "Or the next day."

"Why wait?" Gideon asked. "I'm tired. You're armed. You want me dead and I . . ." He paused. "I'm in the mood for a good scrap."

"I imagine you are," Renny agreed, angling his head towards the retreating Doc while his eyes remained on Gideon's. "But if I kill you now, I won't be able to enjoy how you're suffering." And then, before Gideon, who was indeed suffering, could respond, he turned and walked away.

CHAPTER 5
DAY 29

Gideon wasn't even a month into his sentence when someone took the long walk.

Not that he knew this straightaway. No one even suspected it, until evening roll call, after his work party was lined up next to their crawler.

"Mololo!" CO Tullaine called out.

"Here."

"Escamilla!"

"Bah."

Gideon watched Tullaine look at Pavel, open her mouth, then shake her head and return to the list of the day's party. "Boucher," she called out.

"Always," Renny drawled.

"Quinn!"

"Here."

"Rhouk-Paquin."

"Here, Boss," Nyal said.

"Halili."

Tullaine waited, looked up. "Halili?" she called again,

looking over the long line of convicts, all sporting head-to-toe coats of brick-red dust. "Anyone see Manny Halili?"

Gideon and several others looked up the line, then down, but found no sign of Manny, who had arrived on the same airship as Gideon.

Now, as he and the others began to shift, looking over each other's shoulders for the missing inmate, a good dozen corrections officers closed in to loom over the assembled prisoners, while two more, Menk and Woo, conferred with Tullaine.

After a quick, heated discussion, Woo strode back to the work site, while Menk headed to the cab of the crawler—to radio the prison, Gideon supposed.

"Everyone back in line," Tullaine snapped, turning her attention back to the now-milling prisoners. "Callas," she called out, glancing at the clipboard.

"Yo!" Mama called back.

"Worchowski," Tullaine called out. When the last prisoner pronounced himself present, she jerked a thumb at the crawler. "Everyone load up."

"What about Manny?" Nyal asked.

"Not your problem," Tullaine told him, though, from her expression, Gideon expected it would be her problem if Manny didn't make a hasty appearance.

He didn't, and it wasn't until the end of a subdued dinner hour, which Gideon shared with Nyal, Doc, Lonnie, and Kneecaps, when Warden Simkins appeared at the head of the mess, that Gideon and the others learned what had happened.

"You'll have heard by now that Manny Halili did not return from today's work site," Simkins began, his usually deep voice downright sepulchral. "Once his absence was confirmed, Corrections Officer Woo returned to Halili's assigned work location, where he discovered Halili's crystal canister, spade, and . . ." He paused, swallowed. "And his ear." He waited until the various sounds of swearing, gagging, and dropping of spoons eased.

"Do you have large predators out here?" Gideon murmured.

Nyal, at Gideon's left, shook his head.

"Further investigation revealed a set of footprints, with blood trace, leading to the east. All indications point to Halili doing harm to himself before leaving of his own volition. Following protocol, the staff will not engage in pursuit. Halili is free to continue on his course, and just as free to return. For now, I recommend everyone get a good night's rest, and contemplate the folly of wandering off into the desert."

"Does this happen often?" Gideon asked the others at his table once the warden had departed and the murmurs and rumblings of subdued conversation spurted back to life.

"Not so much," Lonnie said. "But there's some doing hard time who just . . . get tired."

"Manny got here the same time I did," Gideon pointed out. "And he was only sentenced to three years."

"But he's also a sensitive," Nyal said.

"How do you know?" Lonnie asked.

"He told me after I lost the sixteenth game of hangman in a row," Nyal said, poking at his rations with his spoon. He looked at Doc. "Do you think it was him being a sensitive that sent him mad?"

Doc, who was still staring at the space Simkins had occupied, turned his attention back to those at the table. "There's no way of knowing, is there?"

CHAPTER 6
DAY 1561

Time passed.

The suns moved.

Sweat formed, and dried, and formed again over Gideon's skin, and the ever-present thirst left his tongue feeling like sandpaper.

His breath rasped, harsh in his throat, and beneath his boots, the desert grit rattled.

His shadows, twinned like the suns that cast them, angled to his left while, to the north, a glint shimmered from a low rise. Possibly another crystal vein, waiting to be harvested.

It was hot, but it was always hot while Tyche and Nemesis ruled the Barrens.

Eventually, he knew, the suns would sink below the jagged horizon, and then the cold would slide in, sly as a shard dagger in the hands of an enemy.

From somewhere, close or far—one could never tell the way sound traveled in the desert—he heard the rustle of movement.

A scarab, or lizard. Or a mouse, perhaps.

Then another sound, a quick hiss, overtook the rustle.

A brief scuffle and a shorter squeal told Gideon the likely fate of the scarab, or lizard, or mouse.

Since there was smog-all he could do about that—smog-all he could do about anything, really—he fixed his eyes on varying shades of red in front of him and continued to walk.

As he did, a part of his mind kept track of the steps—4,232 . . . 4,233 . . . 4,234—while another part considered that, if he kept his pace up, he might hit the 9,562nd step soon after sunset.

Gideon understood the number of steps claimed to be the difference between returning to captivity and a lonely, thirsty death to be arbitrary, but knowing didn't make the milestone any less stony.

With no guide to speak of, Gideon followed the suns, which were descending towards the toothy ridge of mountains named the Jackal's Fangs.

. . . 4,252 . . .

He didn't so much feel a lessening of heat, but he did feel a trickle of sweat that didn't immediately evaporate, which meant night—and the cold—would eventually overtake him.

. . . 4,253 . . .

His footsteps raised a puff of dust. The dry silicate tickled his nose, and the glittering vein he'd spied to the north curved closer, the spears and spikes of crystal sparking to fire in the late afternoon light.

. . . 4,254 . . .

And as he continued to move, step after step, doggedly making his way towards a jagged ridge he had no hope of ever reaching, he began to feel . . .lighter.

. . . 4,255 . . .

As if, he thought, he was fading away to nothing.

. . . 4,256 . . .

Perhaps that was how it happened, out here.

. . . 4,257 . . .

A body didn't expire so much, just disappeared.

. . . 4,258 . . .

"A pretty thought, for such an ugly business."

. . . 4,25—

Gideon froze, and his heart skipped a beat as he came to a halt mid-count.

For a moment he remained still, then the breath he'd been holding huffed out, and with an aching slowness he turned to the left, where the man who'd just spoken stood.

"Hey, Renny," he said in a voice rusty from dust, disuse, and disbelief.

"Gideon." Eyes, as deep a brown as Gideon remembered, shaded to red in the light of the sinking suns.

Gideon continued to stare. "You should know," he said at last, "I don't believe in ghosts."

"Nor do I," Renny replied, letting his eyes rove over the desert before returning to latch onto Gideon's. "And yet, here we are."

CHAPTER 7
DAY 38

"Officer Kamal . . . Gideon."

Gideon, leaning heavily on the CO, watched Doc rise from his handkerchief-sized desk and gesture to one of the empty cots.

While Doc retrieved a rolling stool and instrument tray, Kamal—a hard-eyed, lean-muscled Fujian—led Gideon to the indicated bed, keeping a bone-crushing grip on Gideon's arm all the way.

"Thanks, Boss," Doc said as the guard shoved Gideon onto the cot.

Gideon managed to squelch the yelp of pain. Mostly.

CO Kamal's lips quirked before they removed themselves to the end of the cot, crossed their arms over their chest, and proceeded to loom.

"May I?" Doc asked, indicating the hand Gideon had pressed against his side.

Gideon lowered his hand so the physician could peel back his bloodstained shirt.

"Nasty," Doc murmured. "From the looks of this wound,

he'll be here at least a day. Possibly two," he said, glancing up at Kamal.

"Work boss'll be thrilled," the CO said, sending Gideon a fulminating glare before they stalked out of the infirmary.

"You have such a way with people," Doc observed as Kamal's footsteps faded away.

"It's a gift."

"Mmm," Doc murmured. "Lie back if you please."

Gideon stretched out on the cot while Doc snapped on a pair of the bio-plastic gloves Gideon recognized from numerous visits to the triage tent.

"I confess myself surprised," the doctor said as he cracked open a clean-and-suture kit. "I was beginning to think I'd never see you in here."

"Why's that?" Gideon asked as he stared up at the ceiling, where he discovered Doc had pinned a series of drawings—some artistic, some comical, and some out-and-out bawdy—above the cots. One even featured a detailed portrait of Elvis Presley, in full royal regalia.

Dani would have been thrilled.

"I had Mama, Pavel, and Lonnie in here a few weeks ago," Doc explained, drawing Gideon's thoughts back to the present, while separating forceps, sutures, and cleansing solutions, "all claiming to have been thoroughly trounced by the Shovel of Hesitation—"

"Spade," Gideon corrected on an exhale. "*Spade* of Hesitation. A shovel has a different shape."

"I stand corrected," Doc replied, turning to move Gideon's shirt out of the way. "*Keepers*," he added, on an exhale of his own.

Gideon, confused, looked down to see Doc glaring at a series of scars decorating his torso.

"War is hell." Gideon offered the blanket explanation.

Better, he thought, than entertaining memories of the Midasian interrogator who'd caused the damage.

"Of course," Doc replied, and while his expression declared he could tell the difference between a wound taken in battle and one received from a specialist in the field, he let the partial-lie lie. "Where was I?" he asked, leaning close to assess the stab wound.

"Spade of hesitation," Gideon told him, fixing his gaze on the drawing above his cot, which appeared to be a replica of the Earth masterpiece, *Dogs Playing Five-Card Apiary*.

"Of course," Doc said, taking up the pair of forceps and probing the wound in search of debris. "A few days after the spade incident, two other inmates came in with lacerations about the face and neck from the, ah, Dinner Tray of Reason?" He glanced up.

"Reason being Sayyed and Jimmy wanted to stick a fork in me to see if I was done," Gideon explained.

Doc's lips twitched as he removed an errant piece of thread from the wound. "And yesterday it was Suleiman DeGuerre, still wet from the showers and suffering from an encounter with the Soapstone of Back the Smog Off."

"I don't think that one needs an explanation," Gideon replied.

"No," Doc agreed, popping open a tube of anti-bac gel. "But the fact is, after such a lengthy string of successes, I can't help but wonder how someone got past your guard to do *this*." As he spoke, he poured the liquid directly into the wound.

"Ouch," Gideon said as foam erupted over his side. "Sadly, the Weighted Sock of Contemplation was no match for Renny's shard," Gideon admitted through gritted teeth.

The doctor looked up. "You lost me."

Gideon withdrew a sock from its hiding place in his sleeve and displayed the gaping hole in that garment's heel. "It blocked

Renny's first stab, but all the gravel leaked out before I got the chance to teach him the value of meditation."

Doc's eyes narrowed at the sight of the abused sock. "I'm sorry to say I'll have to pronounce the hosiery dead on arrival," he said. "Still, better a pierced sock than your heart."

"Renny would probably disagree," Gideon said. "Especially since his shard got tangled in the heel."

"Oh?" Doc said.

Gideon held up a finger before, from behind his back, he produced the gleaming length of Renny's shard.

"Ah," Doc said.

"Yeah." Gideon grinned and snugged the shard into his right sleeve, next to the sock.

"And do you plan on doing unto Renny as he is so desperately trying to do unto you?" Doc asked.

Gideon's lips twisted as Doc rinsed the wound a second time. "No."

"Really?" Doc ripped open the suture pack. "Why not, if you don't mind my asking? Given your past as a soldier, killing would hardly be outside your skill set."

"It isn't," Gideon agreed. "But knowing how to kill—knowing you can—doesn't mean it should be the default."

Doc's brows rose, but he kept his eyes on the work. "An interesting point of view, for a man in the Barrens."

"Maybe I'm reforming," Gideon muttered.

"And only a month into your sentence," Doc observed. "But if you don't mean to end Renny with that little toy, why risk hanging on to it?"

"Mostly to keep it out of Renny's hands, and therefore my back," Gideon said. "And . . ." he paused, hissing, as Doc inserted the first suture, " . . . I have a sort of side project that could use it."

"Ah," Doc said with a nod. "The list."

Gideon started. "You know about that?"

"I work housekeeping in addition to running the infirmary," Doc explained. "I've been in your cell a few times, so I've seen the list. Or the start of it. It appears to be slow going."

"It was," Gideon agreed. "But now I've got myself a better chisel, it'll move along quicker."

"I suppose that's so," Doc agreed. "Though I wonder . . ." But he stopped himself and seemed to focus intensely on getting the exact right angle for the next suture.

"What do you wonder?" Gideon asked.

Doc inserted the suture before he replied. "I wonder why a man serving a life sentence would be in a rush to finish anything."

CHAPTER 8
DAY 110

SOME MONTHS AFTER THE DEATH OF HIS SOCK, GIDEON wandered from his work site to join the rest of the harvesting team for the extended lunch period, a concession to the potentially fatal heat of the midday suns.

Approaching the open-air rations cart from which the meals were distributed, he envisioned a Pavel-sized pizza with a Turing-style crust and every topping known to Fortune.

Okay, every topping except aubergines.

Gideon had staked his tent firmly in the "No Aubergines on Pizza" camp.

Not that it mattered, because while the pizza remained aromatically planted in his imagination, CO Kamal was atop the cart, dispensing the two cups of freeze-dried nutrition pellets and two liters of water every prisoner was allotted during their lunch break.

Gideon accepted his share with inner resignation and an outer "thank you." This was partly because his fagin had raised him to be polite and partly because years in the Corps taught him it paid to be nice to whoever was handing out the grub.

From Kamal's sneer, he doubted the guard was impressed, but old habits were hard to break.

Once he had his bowl and flask, he headed towards a promising patch of shade by a boulder, where he could eat and enjoy the long rest period in peace.

On the way, however, he caught sight of Renny.

The rangy Adian had already collected his rations but, unlike every other member of the work party, he wasn't eating.

Instead, he was staring fixedly at the lunch cart.

Gideon looked back to where Kamal continued to hand out bowl after bowl of ostensible food. But, as they were facing the other way, they didn't notice Renny's rapt attention.

Nor could they see the weaving head of the iridescent white snake pushing its way out of one of the food containers, or the viper's telltale hood flashing wide and white as a moon as it reared high.

Imaginary pizzas faded from Gideon's mind and actual rations flew from his hands as he raced back to the cart.

"Behind you!" he yelled as he ran, a warning which only resulted in Kamal turning to glare at Gideon, their expression darkening and their hand dropping to the hilt of their shock baton.

A series of *k-chunks* from all sides told Gideon at least a few crossbows had been cocked.

Gritting his teeth, he launched himself at Kamal, knocking them off the cart even as a lash of white cut across the air where Kamal had been standing.

Ignoring Kamal's curses, Gideon twisted his body so when they landed, he took the brunt of the fall.

By now, the knocked crossbows were firing, so Gideon twisted again, this time rolling Kamal to the ground to spare them being battered by the rubber-tipped bolts.

"Ow," he said, and then cursed.

"Are you insane?" Kamal asked, glaring up at him, a flush deepening the sepia tones of their complexion.

"Maybe." Gideon cursed again as another bolt struck.

"Hold your fire!" Kamal called out and, as the thudding of rubber on and around Gideon's body ceased, added a terse, "Get. Off."

"Okay," he said, and rolled to one side, his vision blurring with shock as he felt new contusions blossoming every-smog-ging-where. "Ow," he said again, while the thudding of boots and puffs of dust told him more guards were joining the party.

"Time to learn what happens to troublemakers," Gideon heard someone growl, and blinked away some dust to identify CO Kozinski, a recent addition to the Morton security force, moving his foot back.

He was bracing himself for the expected kick when he heard Kamal shout, "Wait!"

"Why?" Kozinski asked.

"Snake," Gideon wheezed, one hand flapping toward the cart.

"A viper," Kamal confirmed, stepping back from the cart with deliberate care. "It must have gotten into the rations."

CO Menk slid a live round into his crossbow before joining Kamal. "How on toxic Earth did a snake get in there?"

Gideon, who'd managed to sit up by now, saw Renny observing the proceedings with a decidedly sour expression, and had a pretty good idea how that snake had gotten into the rations.

A few minutes later, when Renny sidled up to Gideon, who sat hunched over a second bowl of freeze-dried nutrition, his suspicions were confirmed.

"You really are the worst," Renny said, squatting next to Gideon.

"Says the guy who just tried to commit murder by snake," Gideon said, after swallowing a mouthful of kibble.

"Please, that viper wouldn't have killed anyone," Renny scoffed, then paused, considering. "*Probably* it wouldn't have killed anyone."

"And you know this, how?"

"I saw it bite a hyrax before I grabbed it," Renny said. "I'm not suicidal enough to risk handling a viper with full venom sacs."

"Okay," Gideon said, then he paused, thought. "But why?"

"Maybe I wanted everyone looking at the lunch cart instead of me."

"Again, why?"

"Because," Renny hissed, "if everyone was looking at the lunch cart, I'd have had a chance to get into the crystal trolley for a fresh sliver of shard. Which is something I'd never have had to do, if you hadn't stolen my original piece."

"I never stole your shard," Gideon pointed out. "You carelessly left it tangled in my sock."

"I want it back."

"I thought you were going to get a new one?"

"I was, until your heroic leap put one of the guards, and her riot bow, on top of the crystal trolley."

"Ah."

"Where," Renny asked, "is my shard?"

"Somewhere safe," Gideon told him, and when Renny's eyebrows arched meaningfully, added, "It's not on me."

"This is exactly why you don't deserve it," Renny hissed. "I *always* kept it close."

"That's because you're a stone killer."

"I wasn't always," Renny murmured, rising. "But you?" He looked down at Gideon. "You were always a thief."

Before Gideon could ask what he meant by that, Renny had straightened and headed back to the veins.

And as Renny walked away, he began to whistle a song that Gideon soon recognized as the same ditty Hamish Costanza loved so much.

Hearing it set Gideon's teeth on edge, as he just *knew* it'd get stuck in his brain, and he'd likely be humming the smogging thing for a week.

Gideon had been right.

He did get that swarming song stuck in his head.

So stuck that the perky tune, and the memories associated with it, kept him awake several hours past lights out.

Memories of Hamish himself, humming that damned song over a campfire as he doctored the rations, somehow turning the dried aurochs, veg, and pomegranate seeds foraged during the day into a sweet and savory concoction that made Gideon's mouth water even now.

Then there were the recollections of Hamish and Walsie, arguing over their favorite queen teams, or Hamish and Private Lau flirting as he disabled a mine she'd uncovered.

And lastly, of Hamish, standing between Dani and the other surviving members of the Twelfth Company, including Tina Lau, listening as Gideon confessed to treason before the assembled court martial.

It was this last memory that, at long last, followed Gideon into sleep, and, perhaps ironically, away from all his worries.

Because it was here, in dreams, that Gideon could at last leave behind the rigors of the Barrens, the accusatory echoes of the court martial, and experience a moment before the world named him traitor.

A moment when he was still Colonel Gideon Quinn, alone in his quarters back at Epsilon Base.

A moment in which Dani slipped into the room.

In the dream, as in life, Gideon looked up from whatever book he'd been reading at the time to see her shedding her jacket to the floor, followed by her gun belt, boots, trousers, and the rest before sliding under his blanket.

"Mind if I interrupt?" she asked, eying the book.

Her voice had been low, and warm, the Fujian accent adding a hint of mystery.

"Interrupt what?" he'd asked back, letting the book slide down to join her scattered clothing.

From there, the dream progressed much as he recalled, with the catches of breath, the brush of lips, and the weight of Dani's leg sliding across his as she shifted under the blankets.

Which was when Gideon came suddenly, chillingly awake, to find himself staring up at a slim bar of light from the corridor, which bisected the ceiling.

From a distance he heard the steady tread of the night guard, and closer the snores of Pavel, and the muttered curses of Mama, who talked in her sleep.

Gideon had a moment to regret waking—the dream had been remarkably visceral.

So much so, he could still feel the weight of Dani's leg moving over his.

Even as he thought this, her leg shifted again, this time accompanied by a soft rasp, as of something heavy moving over a rough blanket.

Gideon held his breath, and—moving as slowly as possible— lifted his head so he could, in the same faint light spilling from the corridor, spy the moon-white hump slithering up his right leg.

He barely had time to recognize the chill of terror shooting up his spine when the snake reared and its hood flared, prepared to strike.

CHAPTER 9
DAY 111

G IDEON ENTERED THE MESS A FEW MINUTES LATER THAN his usual, but as he strode up to the chow line, he smiled brightly at Mama, who was doling out the rations this morning.

Undaunted by her answering scowl, he collected his tray, which he was grateful to see included a cup of tea alongside the usual water and food rations, and sidled over to join the table where Doc, Nyal, Kneecaps, and Pavel were already seated.

"—has to be goat," Pavel said, facing off with Kneecaps Mololo.

"It's no such thing," Kneecaps replied, waving her spoon in Pavel's face.

Since Kneecaps had gotten her nickname for being notoriously short, and therefore inclined to target her enemy's knees, and Pavel came in full Pavel-size, the confrontation came off looking like a gnat threatening a mammoth.

"You say I am wrong?" Pavel asked, his muddy brown eyes narrowing.

"Morning," Gideon said, drawing both Pavel and Kneecaps from their argument before asking, "has anyone seen Renny yet?"

"I try never to see Renny," Kneecaps groused into her kibble.

"Haven't seen him," Nyal said with a shrug.

"Why?" Doc asked, with noticeable suspicion.

"No reason," Gideon said, sliding into the space between Nyal and Pavel. "So, what are we arguing about?" he asked, while slipping a small stack of spent matches in Nyal's direction.

"Oh, thanks," Nyal said, sliding the matches—which Gideon knew he was using to build the Nike clock tower—into his pocket. "We're trying to guess which protein was used in today's rations," he said, in answer to Gideon's question. "It's different from the usual factory chicken."

"I am saying it is goat," Pavel said.

"And I'm telling you it's out-and-out soy," Kneecaps countered.

"What's your take?" Gideon asked Nyal.

"I was thinking almond paste," Nyal said.

"Almond is too smogging pricey," Kneecaps told him.

Gideon looked at Doc.

"I have no hive in this meadow," the medic said.

"It's soy," Kneecaps insisted.

"You try," Nyal said to Gideon.

"Okay," Gideon agreed, then dug in with his spoon to take a bite of the disputed kibble. He held the freeze-dried pellets on his tongue for a moment, savoring the nutty essence as they softened.

"Well?" Kneecaps pressed.

Gideon held up a "just a second" finger, closed his eyes, chewed and, at last, swallowed. He opened his eyes, saw the others all staring at him. "It's not vat-grown goat," he said.

"Told you!" Kneecaps said.

"It's not soy, or almond either," Gideon cautioned, tapping his spoon on the side of his bowl. "It's cricket."

"No way," Kneecaps said, then tasted another spoonful and frowned. "Huh," she said.

Pavel was also chewing, his face scrunched in what Gideon took to be a thoughtful expression.

"How can you tell?" Nyal asked, poking at the remains of his own breakfast.

"Some of my missions strayed pretty far from the usual supply lines, so we had to forage, or starve," Gideon told him. "One of my company had a dab hand with toasted crickets," he added, once again thinking of Hamish Costanza, who, besides being a connoisseur of terrible music, could also cook anything you put in front of him.

Wonder what he's up to these days, he wondered to himself.

Hopefully not eating dehydrated cricket, his self responded.

Accepting this was not a fruitful route of inquiry, he dug into his kibble and listened as the chatter moved from the breakfast menu to the panto Lonnie meant to put on that evening, if his cast wasn't too knackered from a day in the veins.

He was about halfway through the bowl, and Nyal was just finishing his review of Lonnie's last directorial effort, when Renny finally appeared.

To Gideon's eye, the Adian appeared agitated, and his dark eyes flashed murderously as they aimed in his direction.

In response, Gideon smiled and raised his spoon in a toast before turning back to his meal.

He was just taking a slow, appreciative sip of his tea when Renny slid into the spot to Doc's left.

"Doc," Renny said, then looked across the table. "Gideon. You look . . . rested."

"Renny," Gideon set his mug down. "You look like you've seen a viper."

As the antagonists' eyes locked, Kneecaps rolled her own before picking up her tray and making for the dish-washing line.

"Funny you should mention," Renny said to Gideon. "Oddest thing, but when I woke up this morning, there was a viper draped over the foot of my cot."

"First crickets, now snakes." Pavel took his tray and departed for less graphic waters.

"Keepers!" Nyal said.

Doc let out a long-suffering sigh.

"A viper?" Gideon asked. "You mean, like the one with the white scales, and the hood that does this?" He put his hands to either side of his head and exploded them out.

"The very same," Renny said.

"Wow." Gideon shook his head. "You're lucky to be alive."

"Very lucky," Renny agreed, "as the viper turned out to be dead."

"Eww," was Nyal's pronouncement.

Gideon leaned on his elbows and peered at Renny. "So, you're saying a desert viper came slithering into your cell and just up and kicked it on your cot?"

"I suspect its neck was broken," Renny said. "Before or after its head was smashed. It's hard to say, really."

"Ack," Nyal said, then looked at Doc, who was choking. "You okay, Doc?"

"Wrong pipe," Doc gasped, rising from the table with his tray. "I'll just go find some water," he added hoarsely.

Gideon turned his attention back to Renny. "Maybe it was trying to slither up the wall and just . . . dropped on its head?"

"From the looks of the thing, it would have had to have dropped a few dozen times," Renny said.

"Huh." Gideon thought. "Maybe it slithered up the wall and fell a few dozen times."

Renny's eyes narrowed. "And why would a viper do such a stupid thing?"

Gideon's lip curled. "Maybe it's a really stupid viper who never learns from its mistakes."

"You know, I don't think snakes actually have necks," Nyal observed.

"Excuse me?" Renny turned to the young man.

"You said its neck was broken, but I don't think they have necks, as such. I mean, aren't they all neck?" As Nyal spoke, he sketched a long, sinuous shape with his spoon. "And I don't think they have bones, really. They're more like cartilage." Then he lowered the spoon and looked from Gideon to Renny and back to Gideon. "You know what?" he said, shoving up from the table, "I think Doc needs—I mean, I think I should go check on Doc."

"Good idea," Gideon agreed, but Nyal was already halfway to the table where Doc had settled after his strategic retreat.

Gideon turned his attention back to Renny.

"How did you get a dead viper into my cell before the morning bell?" Renny asked.

"Friends in high places," Gideon said, thinking of CO Kamal, who'd been on night watch, then he focused on Renny. "How did you get a live viper into my cell, after lights out?"

"Friends in low places," Renny replied, glancing towards the door of the mess, where CO Kozinski leaned against the wall, eying the inmates with a bored expression.

"That *is* low," Gideon agreed, then leaned in even closer as Renny took a sip of tea. "How about we try this? You tell me why you hate me so I can apologize and we can both move on?"

"Do you know what's funny about that?" Renny asked, setting down his mug and picking up his spoon. "What's funny about that is how you believe any apology would ever be enough."

CHAPTER 10
DAY 1561

In the middle of the desert, Gideon licked lips long gone dry. He glanced up at the suns, creeping ever closer to the horizon, then looked back to confirm that the apparition of Renny Boucher was still standing at his side.

"I can see this is a lot to process," Renny said.

"It would be," Gideon said, "but since neither of us believe in you, I think I'll skip the processing and just," he gestured vaguely forward, "move on." Suiting action to word, he took a step, then paused.

Had he been at 4,261, or 4,262?

With a grimace, he opted to err on the side of caution and start at 4,261.

"Actually, you were at four thousand, two hundred fifty-nine."

Gideon stopped to look at Renny. "Do spirits read minds?"

"Perhaps," Renny said, lips pursed as he mused. "But since neither of us believe in ghosts, it may be I am nothing more than a hallucination, in which case I would know everything you know, because you made me up."

"And why would I do that?" Gideon asked, hands flying out

in frustration. "Of all the people on Fortune, why would I decide to see *you*?"

"Perhaps it's to do with our unfinished business?" Renny suggested.

"Our business is dead and buried," Gideon said, and started to walk again.

... 4,259 ...

... 4,260 ...

... 4,261 ...

"Dead, of a certainty," Renny agreed, skipping to catch up.

CHAPTER 11
DAY 392

SEVERAL MONTHS AFTER THE VIPER EXCHANGE, GIDEON strode out into the middle of the yard, much as he'd done exactly one year ago.

And he knew it had been exactly one year because he'd just been walked out of his first annual parole review.

More like his first annual pointless exercise, he thought, since his alleged crime had earned him a life sentence.

But thanks to the first landers, who were determined not to repeat the mistakes of their Terran forebears, the Colonial criminal justice system required an annual evaluation for each inmate.

Even inmates who'd confessed to treason, and had a snowball's chance in Nasa of ever being released.

Which Gideon had known, going into the meeting, and therefore not the reason he now stood in the center of the yard, silently engaged in a battle to suppress the rage he could feel burning through every molecule.

It had kindled soon after walking into the room and seeing only a token assembly that included Warden Simkins, some pallid lieutenant attached to the Corps Advocate General, and a staff recorder.

The session opened with Lieutenant Spud-face reading out the summary of Gideon's crimes, as well as the transcript of his confession.

It ended with Simkins agreeing solemnly with Spud's assessment that Gideon was a very bad person and slaving away in the veins day in and day out was too good for him.

That CO Kamal was in the room and seemed sympathetic to Gideon's cause somehow made the whole thing worse.

But what *really* twisted the knife—in Gideon's eyes, at least—wasn't the sentence itself, or the way Simkins and the potato bandied their opinions about Gideon as if he weren't even there.

It was, rather, the realization he'd been in the Barrens for an entire year.

Three hundred ninety-two days had passed since he'd first stumbled into the yard, his hand stinging from the prison tattoo and his mind numb with loss.

"Not feeling celebratory?" A too-familiar voice slid through the dark haze, exactly as it had a year ago.

"Not today, Renny," Gideon said.

"But it's your anniversary," an undeterred Renny replied. "We should mark it in some way. Like you marked mine by breaking my nose." He gently touched the bridge of that abused organ, still slightly crooked.

Since he'd only broken Renny's nose because Renny was attempting to strangle him with a bootlace, Gideon opted not to respond.

"Well, if you don't want to celebrate your anniversary, maybe we should raise a bowl of kibble to mark the completion of that swarming list on your wall."

At that, Gideon's lip curled. "What makes you think I've finished?"

"I made some enquiries into your case," Renny said. "Enough to know how many of your company died. Six dead, six names on the wall. Which means," Renny continued, "you've no more need of my shard."

Gideon's gaze slid towards Renny. "And you think I should give it back?"

"It would be the decent thing."

"You just want to bury it in my spine."

"I was thinking more your throat."

"I think I'll hang on to it a bit longer," Gideon decided, and returned to his study of the yard. Less because he was interested in the evening activities and more because he still very much wanted to hit something, and Renny made such an appealing target.

Almost immediately, his eyes landed on Doc, seated at his favorite stone slab. With him were Mama, Suleiman, and a newcomer; a Campbell Islander named Cassandra O'Malley.

Gideon didn't know what Cassandra was in for, but he had seen her in Renny's presence once or twice.

As she flashed a lightning-bright smile at Doc, Gideon could see why Renny would talk her up. Though it was just as likely Renny only wanted to recruit the new inmate in his campaign against Gideon as for any amorous purposes.

With some regret, Gideon continued to scan the yard, fixing next on the vision of Lonnie, sprawled on the ground, rather like a fallen aurochs, with Kneecaps kneeling at his side, and Vito standing over him, clutching a hand to his heart.

Gideon grimaced at what must have been a rehearsal for one of Lonnie's productions, and turned to the net the queen game going forward, just in time to see Pavel chuck the queen past the keeper with a swift smack of his stick.

As Pavel's team whooped with glee, Gideon spied two

figures on the far side of the pitch, both pressed into the shadows of the outer wall.

"Hello?" Renny said, as Gideon angled for a better look. "You do realize I'm still here?"

"Don't care," Gideon said as he recognized one of the two bodies as CO Kozinski, who must have flipped on his shock baton, because a flash of sparks erupted to push back the shadows.

And in that brief flash, Gideon spied a thoroughly petrified Nyal, pushing himself into the wall.

Gideon was moving before he knew it.

"Wait," he heard Renny say.

"No," he responded, and kept moving.

"You're going to get killed," Renny hissed, following.

"Isn't that what you want?" Gideon asked.

"Only if I'm involved," Renny replied, then clammed up as both men came up alongside Doc's card game.

"What's going on?" Doc asked, glancing up and then following the direction of Gideon's glare.

"Ah, well. Will you look at that?" The older man huffed his disapproval.

The comment had the rest of the players looking up from the cards in time to see Kozinski holding Nyal by the collar while he waved the baton in front of the young man's glassy eyes.

Gideon's lip curled, and he spared Renny a glance. "When you speak of this—and you know you will—be specific."

"What?" Doc asked, looking from Gideon to Renny and back to Nyal's dilemma. "Speak of what?"

"It's a short story," Renny replied. "I believe I will call it *The Death of an Idiot.*"

Gideon didn't bother responding as he worked his way to

his objective, using the shove-and-tumble of the queen game to cover his approach.

All the while, he kept his eyes on Kozinski, repeatedly tapping his baton against the wall, sparking and sparking again as he brought the charged stick ever closer to the trembling Nyal.

"—just saying," Gideon heard the CO say as he drew close, "a little friendliness could go a long, long way to making your life easier. Or you could keep being *unfriendly* and find out just how hard things can get."

The stick sparked closer, and closer, and was perilously near Nyal's head when Gideon slid in to wind his arm around Kozinski's.

"What the hel-*eeoww*!" The guard's exclamation accompanied Gideon's circling action, which dragged the baton away from Nyal's face and towards Kozinski's.

In self-defense, Kozinski dropped the weapon, which fell, sparks shooting everywhere as it bounced and rolled to a stop at the foot of the wall. "Quinn?" he sputtered, trying to free the arm Gideon still had entangled. "Are you insane?"

"People keep asking me that," Gideon replied, and then he punched Kozinski, easing back from the eruption of red from the bulbous nose.

From all around, he heard the low rumble of interest. "*Scarp*," he hissed at Nyal, and was relieved to see the kid fade into the audience gathering on the queen pitch.

Then Kozinski let out a hoarse growl, warning Gideon to dodge an incoming fist, so it only glanced off his ribs.

Gideon growled himself, and with a sense of satisfaction he knew he'd regret later, buried his own fist in Kozinski's throat.

"*Renny owes you*," he muttered as the CO dropped, gasping, to his knees.

At the same time, a series of whistles told Gideon the other screws had taken notice of the scuffle.

On the wall, shouts preceded the appearance of COs' crossbows at the ready, while on the ground, a small army of guards stormed the yard.

From his initial attack to the first whistle, Gideon figured the entire altercation had only lasted about fifteen seconds, but as he looked at the whimpering Kozinski at his feet, he found himself wishing for more time.

At least Nyal had made it to safety, which was more than Gideon could hope for, as the incoming COs surrounded him to apply their own shock batons, as well as a few well-placed boots.

Even as his fists curled, Kamal's barely audible "Don't fight" tickled his ear.

Gideon would never know why, but that single exhortation from the CO managed to do what dreaming of murdering Renny—or *actually* pounding on Kozinski—couldn't.

Because the second he heard the hiss of an order, the rage that had shadowed him into the yard fell away, and only Gideon . . . tired, empty, and alone . . . remained.

How long he would remain, however, was another story, as fists, batons, and boots worked him over until his vision blurred and he wondered if, maybe, the guards really *were* going to do Renny's work for him.

Which was when he heard CO Kamal's voice ordering everyone to stand down, and beyond that, a low, repetitive thumping he couldn't identify.

Squinting through the pain, dust, and tears, he could just make out the mass of prisoners standing in a distant circle, and how each and every one of them was pounding a fist to the heart, over and over and over in an echo of the hand to the heart of the Colonial Corps.

And just as the whisper of warning earlier had deprived him

of his close-held rage, this voiceless tribute rushed in to fill the vacancy with something else—a something he'd never have expected to feel in this place.

He could only hope, as Kamal and Menk hauled him to his feet, that this new sense of belonging would sustain him for what was likely to be a long, uncomfortable stint in solitary.

No one could have been more surprised than Gideon when that stint turned out to be only a few hours.

And it turned out to be only a few hours because CO Kamal hadn't accepted Kozinski's story—that it had been Gideon who'd been threatening Nyal, and who turned on Kozinski when the guard tried to intervene.

Kamal had followed through on their hunch by first speaking to Nyal, and then a number of other prisoners who'd witnessed the beat-down, including Doc himself, and Renny.

Once they'd gotten the story from the inmates, Kamal had gone to the warden, who then did the needful and dismissed Kozinski for cause.

All of this Gideon discovered when he'd been removed from the darkness of the solitary cell and deposited in the infirmary.

"You're telling me a guard went to the wall for a convict?" Gideon asked.

"The same guard you saved from a viper," Doc pointed out.

"Yeah, but—Nyal?" he asked, wincing as Doc prodded a contusion on his back. "He really told the truth about Kozinski?"

"Never seen him so worked up," Doc murmured. "There's a laceration here. May need stitches."

"And Simkins actually gave Kozinski the boot?"

Doc pulled out his suture kit. "Simkins can be a bit pedantic, but he does like to run a clean prison. And another benefit," he added, "Cassandra, the new inmate, was so impressed with your attack of Kozinski, she's given Renny the cold shoulder. So it appears there's one less shard in the back for you to worry over."

"Always a good day when someone doesn't want to kill me," Gideon decided, then cursed as the Doc put in the first suture.

CHAPTER 12
DAY 404

It had been over a week since the confrontation with Kozinski when Gideon decided to retire to his cell early.

He wasn't tired, particularly. Nor was he suffering overmuch from his injuries.

The truth was, Gideon was feeling more than a little oppressed by the admiration of his fellow convicts who, he'd soon discovered, could be remarkably effusive in their support for one of their own sticking it to the man.

So rather than face another evening in the yard, listening to exaggerated recounts of his confrontation with Kozinski, Gideon opted to spend his free time rereading the first two-thirds of *The First Landing: A Tale of Fortune*.

The last third of the book was rumored to be floating around A block, but since Gideon had a pretty good idea how that first landing turned out (Spoiler! The Earthers set up housekeeping on Fortune and got busy), he didn't much mind being left on a cliffhanger.

He was just drawing the battered chapters from under his pillow when he sensed the presence of another.

"If you're after your shard, Renny," he said wearily, "it's not in here." *At least, it's not here today,* he thought, because one of the reasons Renny could never find the shard was that Gideon continually changed the hiding place.

"I'm not Renny, and I can promise, 'tisn't *his* shard I'm after."

Turning, Gideon found himself face-to-face with Cassandra, the new inmate he'd seen playing cards with Doc. "Ah," he said, then added, "hi." Then he took a step away because, in Gideon's experience, most people who snuck up behind a body were inclined to stab that body in the back.

"Hi," she said back. "Care for a cuppa?"

He frowned, looked around, as if a kettle would turn up out of the ether. "I don't have any tea in here at the moment. Or ever."

"Fordians," she muttered, rolling eyes he now noticed were blue. "'Tis a metaphor, Quinn."

"For what?" He took another step back as she stepped forward.

"For this," she said, grabbing hold of his shirt and hauling him close.

"Oh," Gideon said, before getting involved in the kiss. When they both came up for air, he was grinning. "I never metaphor I didn't like," he said.

At the pun, *she* stepped back. "Are you going to keep doing that?"

"Not if you don't want me to." Had he noticed the freckles dotting her golden-brown skin before? He didn't think so.

"I don't," she said firmly.

"Then, no."

"Good."

"Only," he held up a cautioning hand as she eased closer, "we're still a few weeks out from the monthly conjugal allowance."

Her head tipped. "Seeing as we're both of us in the stir, I'd say it follows neither of us are all that keen on following rules." Even as she was pointing this out, Cassandra was busy unbuttoning his shirt. "You've a fine body," she murmured, running her hands over it. "I like that it's seen some action."

"Some," Gideon agreed, but as her hands moved south, he grasped her wrists to hold them in place. "Before things get involved, I'd like to know if you're planning on stabbing me."

Her gaze flicked up. "Why on Fortune would I want to be stabbing you?"

"I don't know," he admitted. "But people often do."

"I don't want to stab you," she assured him.

"Okay, but—"

"If you don't want to enjoy a cuppa, you've only to say." Then her lips quirked, bringing out unexpected dimples. "But I'll know you're lying."

"Ha," he managed. "And not saying no. But we only have twenty minutes, tops, before Menk makes his next round of the floor."

Her lips quirked. "Then we'd best work quick, hadn't we?"

Their eyes met, locked, and then they dove at one another with a shared urgency that neither asked, nor gave, any quarter.

Some minutes later—close to the twenty he'd calculated, given they could hear Menk's droning whistle from the floor below—Gideon and Cassandra parted.

He looked over her shoulder at the cell door. "We should—"

"You," she cut him off, "are a fecking idiot."

"What?" Gideon tried to sit up, but she was still lodged on top of him. "I'm a—*what*?"

"An idiot." She punched his chest even as he shot up, allowing her to slide off the cot.

"About what?" he demanded while she set about buttoning her shirt.

She shook her head, then hissed and looked at him before uttering a single word. "*Nasa*."

Gideon let out a pained hiss of his own. "You're a sensitive," he deduced as she dropped next to him to slip on her socks.

"A contact reader," she confirmed. "Takes skin to skin for me to really get a look—and in the throes, as it were, it's a smogging big window." She slid a foot into one boot, glanced at him through a coiling explosion of gilded hair. "Fecking idiot."

"A sensitive," he said again.

"Idiot." She slid on the other boot before popping to her feet.

"Does the prison staff know?" he asked, rolling off the bed to pull on his own clothing. "About your sensitivity, I mean?"

"Of course they know." She began to tuck in her shirt. "Why do you think I'm in the smogging Barrens in the first place?"

"I have no idea," he admitted.

"So much for my dreams of fame," she huffed. "The short version is that I was a licensed member of the night trade."

Gideon, still recovering from the last few minutes, whistled. "You must have been rolling in starbucks."

"Flatterer." Her smile made a brief appearance. "I did well enough, but the competition in Nike's Red Crystal Alley is fierce. And I wanted . . . more."

"Ah."

"Mmm," she agreed, watching him button his trousers. "And, seeing a way to get more, I used my talent to dig a little deeper than required for the pleasure of my clients. I stole their secrets," she explained as Gideon looked up. "Some they paid me to keep, some I sold to the highest bidder, and some I passed on to members of the shadow trade, for a cut of the take."

"Okay," he said, then thought about what she'd just learned from him. "Are you planning to use my secret against me?"

At that, she laughed. "And what swarming good would that do me?" she asked, waving a hand at the idea. "Sadly, there's no profit to be made from spilling the fact that you lied when you confessed to treason. Idiot."

"Thank you," he said, too grateful to mind the insult. Then, as he tucked in his shirt, added, "You know, you shouldn't be in the Barrens."

"The Nike constabulary would disagree," she said with another bubble of laughter as she eyed him. "I'm not sure how to break this to you, but I am *not* a nice person."

"This was nice," he said.

"This was for my pleasure, and a pleasure it was," she told him. "But it's for certain sure you'd never find me putting meself between me mates and a firing squad the way you did."

"Still," he said, clearing his throat, "the Barrens is not a good place for people like you."

"Oh, I've heard the stories," she said with a shrug. "But it seems to me that a body would need to have some serious talent for a wee buzzing bit of crystal to be a problem. Being but a touch sensitive, I should be fine." She leaned in to deliver what he supposed she meant to be a reassuring kiss, then shook her head as she straightened. "Don't do that."

"Do what?" he asked, focusing intently on buttoning his shirt.

"Don't be adding me to the list of people you think need saving," she told him, with a poke to the shoulder.

"*Ow.*"

"I mean it, Gideon," she said. "I've only to last the three years. And if things go swarm, well," she shrugged. "Maybe that's a kind of justice?"

"I wouldn't have thought you cared about justice."

"And so I don't. Meanwhile, I'll thank you for your concern.

And for this," she said, glancing at the rumpled cot and back. "Especially as we'll not be doing it again."

"We won't?"

Her smile flashed. "You're entirely too honorable for the likes of me, Gideon Quinn." And with that, and a small sigh, she turned towards the cell door at the same time CO Menk appeared in the open rectangle.

"What's all this, then?" Menk asked.

"Just enjoying a cuppa," Cassandra said with a wink.

Both Menk and Gideon watched with appreciation as she sauntered out of the cell.

As her footsteps faded, Menk turned to Gideon, who braced himself for another round of payback, but was surprised when the guard did nothing more but muster a sneer before turning and continuing on his rounds.

Maybe Kamal had somehow persuaded their peers to lay the smog off.

Gideon tried to be grateful for the reprieve, but his entire being was still shaking from the last half hour, and the secrets bared during those desperate minutes of intimacy.

With a huff of breath, he turned to study the six names he'd just finished carving into the wall of his cell.

Each name belonged to a member of his company, killed at Nasa.

Each death had been attributed to Gideon Quinn's treason.

But, as Cassandra now knew, Gideon was not a traitor.

Cassandra, with her intelligent eyes and wicked grin, who claimed she wasn't that much of a sensitive.

Then, for the first time in months, he thought of Manny, who had walked away from the veins without anyone noticing, and never returned.

CHAPTER 13
DAY 405

THE NEXT DAY, GIDEON WENT IN SEARCH OF DOC, WHO HE found idling in the shade of the yard's west wall, shuffling a worn deck of cards.

"Do you remember when you said there was no knowing if Manny being a sensitive had anything to do with his taking the walk?" Gideon asked.

Doc looked up. "And hello to you too."

"But," Gideon continued, "everyone around here says it's the sensitives who go crystal mad most often."

"And of course, 'everyone around here' would be experts in the varied neurological and psychological responses to the proximity of living crystal," Doc replied, carefully setting the cards to one side.

"Okay, maybe we won't count the opinions of the Pavels of the world," Gideon said as he parked himself on the warm slab of rock next to the physician, "but most of the inmates, and a few of the guards, think that the majority of people who *do* go swarm are sensitives of some type or another."

"Which is not impossible," Doc granted. "But it could as easily be presumed that the sensitives in question succumbed from living in proximity with dozens of violent offenders for long periods of time. I'm guessing you hadn't thought of that?" Doc asked, as Gideon frowned.

"I . . . no."

"So few do," Doc murmured. "I imagine it would be difficult enough for those who sense the thoughts or emotions of others to maintain a sense of self in the best of circumstances."

"And these are hardly the best of circumstances," Gideon said, gazing over the yard, his eyes sliding over Nyal, who was sketching something in the air with his hands as he spoke to Lonnie, then over to Pavel and Kneecaps, who seemed to be arguing over the measurements of the queen pitch.

There was Cassandra walking out the kinks of the day along with Mama, who Gideon knew to be dealing with the onset of arthritis. "So if someone's only, say, a contact sensitive, they might have a better chance of getting out whole?"

"I appreciate you may wish to help Cassandra out after your interlude," Doc began.

"Wait," Gideon interrupted, "how do you know about that?"

"You know how the buzz travels here," Doc said pityingly. "I'd say everyone knows about yesterday's tryst by now."

"It's not about what happened yesterday," Gideon began. "Okay, maybe a little about that," he amended as Doc's eyebrows rose. "But she made it clear it was a one-time deal, so mostly it's about wanting to keep another person from wandering off into the desert."

"I understand that," Doc said, "and very much sympathize, but you're asking me to speculate without sufficient data."

"You've been in for, what, six years?" Gideon asked. "How not sufficient can your data be?"

"Yes," Doc replied, his mild voice taking on the barest of edges. "And in that time, I've known five inmates to take the walk, including Manny. Another became uncontrollably violent, and was 'shipped off to an asylum for the cogs to deal with, and one last fell into a catatonic state and was also sent away. Of those seven," he continued, "only three were known to be sensitives. Even taking into account that there are many levels of sensitivity, and not every sensitive is identified, there have not been enough demonstrated instances of acute psychological breaks in the general population over the past six years for me to draw any useful conclusions."

"So there's nothing anyone will do?" Gideon challenged once he'd digested most of what Doc said. "People are going crazy, but everyone just shrugs and moves on because they're criminals and they deserve it?"

"I don't believe—" Doc began.

"Because if pain and suffering is really what all this is about," Gideon cut in, waving at the inmates dotting the yard, "then the Colonies may as well lay down arms and call ourselves Midasians."

"Is that what happened to you?" Doc asked as Gideon's arm dropped. "The scars," he clarified. "Did they come from a Midasian?"

"We're not talking about me," Gideon replied flatly.

Doc said nothing, but his quirked eyebrow spoke volumes.

"If you're thinking I committed treason because I was turned by a Midasian torturer, you're looking for pollen in a barren meadow," Gideon said.

"There'd be no shame in it, if that was what happened."

"Yes, there would," Gideon disagreed. "But it's not what happened. I'm here because I made a choice." Which, as Cassandra now knew, was *a* truth, if not *the* truth. "Meanwhile, back to my original question. Shouldn't someone in power care that so many sensitives are going swarm down here?"

"I couldn't say." As he spoke, Doc picked up his deck of

cards and rose from the warmth of the stone seat. "Perhaps you should ask someone who is in power," he suggested, before walking away and leaving Gideon with the distinct sensation that *couldn't say* wasn't the same as *didn't know.*

Huffing out a soft curse, Gideon's eyes instinctively sought Cassandra, still wandering the yard, just as Mama said something that had Cassandra tossing back her head in a full-out laugh.

Whatever her crimes, Gideon didn't want to see her suffer the same fate as Manny.

Before he could talk himself out of it, he launched himself to his feet, aiming for the nearest CO.

Twenty minutes later he stalked back into the yard, Simkins's reprimands still ringing in his ears.

" . . . what makes you think I'd believe anything a confessed traitor has to say . . ."

" . . . Cassandra O'Malley's actions led to the financial ruin of dozens, and at least two deaths can be traced to the secrets she shared . . ."

" . . . all beside the point that not a single boffin has proved that crystal has any lasting effect on sensitives . . ."

While the basso echoes bounced around in his brain, Gideon scanned the yard, seeking Doc, but, for once, the physician was nowhere to be found.

CHAPTER 14
DAY 433

GIDEON COULDN'T SAY WHAT DROVE HIM TO DO IT.

Maybe it was the uncertainty of how the interlude with Cassandra had ended.

Maybe it was the bitter taste the confrontation with Simkins had left in his mouth.

Or maybe, just maybe, he needed something solid to push against—something more predictable and less ambiguous than crystal madness or a flawed justice system.

Whatever the reason, nearly a month after failing to help Cassandra (*Who*, his self reminded him, *hadn't asked for his help*), Gideon took Renny's shard from its latest hiding place (a hollow under the compost heap) and made his move.

He waited until free time was nearing an end before approaching Renny, who'd just lost a game of Turing Hold 'Em to Doc.

"I know you're cheating," Renny said with disgust as the older man scooped up the loose pages from various newspapers that had made up the pot.

"I never cheat," Doc promised. "But to ease your mind, I'll

return the papers after I've read them." As he spoke, he patted the sheets into a neat pile and looked at Gideon. "Fancy a game?"

"Sorry," Gideon said, "I have nothing left to lose at this point."

"I beg to differ," Renny said, rising from the stone slab Doc used as his table. "I believe you have about five liters of blood to spare."

"Less than two," Doc said, already perusing the top news sheet. "Any more would prove fatal."

"Yes," Renny said, rolling his eyes, "that would be the point."

"Hmm," Doc said, but Gideon could see he was engrossed in his newly won reading material. A quick peek over Doc's shoulder showed an advert for pineapple leather wellies, and an article about the expansion of the Tenjin Corporation's Research and Development division.

Since Doc was already deep into the article, Gideon looked at Renny and jerked his chin towards the northwest wall, which was the darkest of the yard. "A word?"

Renny's eyes narrowed, but then he shrugged. "Why not?" But as he rose, he turned back to Doc. "I hope you like the story about the Dionysus Festival. Looks like the Upanishads won."

"As long as it's not Hamlet," Doc said with equanimity

"Does nothing rile the man?" Renny complained as he followed Gideon across the yard.

Gideon glanced back to where Doc continued to devour the newspapers. "Do you think he did it?" he asked, in lieu of an answer.

"Kill his wife?" Renny also spared Doc a glance. "Doesn't seem the type, but it only takes a moment, doesn't it, to make a choice that can't be unchosen?"

"So I've heard." Since they'd reached their destination, Gideon came to a halt. "Don't suppose you'll finally share which of my choices has you wanting my head on a platter?"

"Don't suppose I will," Renny replied. "And if that's all you wanted to talk about, I've got better things to do than share oxygen with you."

"It isn't," Gideon said, holding out his hand in a "wait a minute" gesture while he took another look around, and then up at the walls to make sure no guards were looking their way.

"What are you at, Gideon?"

Convinced they were, for the moment, unwatched, Gideon looked at Renny. "This," he said, and produced Renny's shard from under his shirt.

"Careful," Renny murmured, his body shifting to a ready stance. "Simkins doesn't take kindly to murder among the inmates."

"That's never stopped you from trying," Gideon pointed out.

"But I'm a stone killer," Renny observed. "You said so yourself."

"And you called me a thief," Gideon said, recalling one of their more contentious conversations.

"Because you are," Renny said, pointing to the shard, "as the evidence suggests."

"Again, I didn't steal it," Gideon reiterated the old argument. "You left it in my sock."

"And I suppose you now plan to leave it in my liver?"

"That would be the smart thing, wouldn't it?" Gideon replied, before flipping the shard in his hand and presenting it, hilt first, to Renny.

Renny gaped, an expression Gideon found oddly refreshing. "You truly are insane, aren't you?"

"I'm starting to think so," Gideon admitted, then dropped his voice to add a low, *"Incoming."*

Renny might not have trusted Gideon, but he took the shard, disappearing it even as the footsteps above came to a halt.

"Everything good down there?"

Gideon recognized the voice as belonging to the newest CO, an Avonian named Finch, brought in to replace the terminated Kozinski.

"All good," he called up, eying Renny. "Isn't it?"

"Everything's honey in the comb," Renny said, but once Finch continued on his rounds, the Adian fixed his dark gaze on Gideon. "This doesn't make us friends."

"Color me shocked," Gideon said dryly, then asked, "Did you want to take a stab at me now?"

"Every minute of every day," Renny said with his thin smile. "But as neither of us is going anywhere—for possibly ever—I don't imagine there's any rush."

"Okay." Gideon remained where he stood, watching Renny, who was watching him.

"You're not leaving?" Renny asked.

"After you," Gideon said, gesturing grandly towards the yard.

Renny grimaced. "I just said I wasn't going to stab you."

"So you did," Gideon agreed, and remained where he was.

Renny stared at Gideon.

Gideon stared at Renny.

"Someone has to move," Renny said.

"You're right." Gideon nodded. "Someone does."

Neither moved.

Finally, the evening bells rang, summoning the inmates back to their cells.

Gideon and Renny continued to stare until Renny heaved a sigh heavy with disgust. "Together, then?"

"In five, four, three, two," Gideon counted down, and on *one,* both men spun on their heels and strode across the yard, side by side.

As they moved, their steps were in synch, and their postures so relaxed, anyone who didn't know the pair might have thought them friends.

CHAPTER 15
DAY 1561

· · · 5,332 · · ·

· · · 5,333 · · ·

· · · 5,334 · · ·

"I don't know if you're aware," Renny said, kicking a rock past Gideon, "but all the cogs say it's unhealthy to keep your emotions bottled up like this."

"I guess that makes you Fortune's healthiest psychopath," Gideon muttered.

"Oh, sting," Renny said, clutching at his heart. "Also, watch your step."

"What?" Gideon asked, even as his toe caught on something sticking out of the ground.

Too spent to fight for balance, he fell flat out, his hands slapping onto the heated sand. He saved himself from a full-on faceplant, but his palms and forearms stung with the effort of catching his weight, and the bark of surprise caused his dried lips to split.

Tasting blood, he raised his head with a grimace and found himself facing, not Renny's smirk, but the fleshless grin of a human skull, half-buried in the sand.

"Ack!" Gideon pushed off from his much-abused hands with enough force to send him flopping all the way in the other direction, to land on his back.

Renny's face appeared directly over his. "Graceful," was the hallucinaghost's opinion.

"Smog off," Gideon replied, sitting up and scooting back to lean against one of the several boulder-sized rocks that decorated the area. Possibly the owner of the skull had stopped here to rest, never to rise.

"You used to be a lot more fun to torture," Renny said, poking a toe at the thigh bone Gideon had tripped over.

"If you're bored, feel free to haunt someone else."

"That might work, if I were actually a ghost, and supposing there was anyone I hated enough." As he spoke, Renny squatted down on the far side of the skeleton. "Since I'm not and there isn't, how about you tell Uncle Renny why you decided to take the long walk?"

Gideon's eyes slid over. "I'd think it'd be enough for you to know I did."

"Please. This barely scratches the levels of suffering I wished on you." Renny eased back against his side of the boulder. "There was one fantasy, for instance, that involved you being staked over a scorpion pit. I had another where a silica worm took up residence in your brain. And of course, the most entertaining, the image of a viper sliding up your trousers to give you a right good bite in the ba—oh, *do* grow up," he said, cutting himself off when the finger bone Gideon threw at him *poinged* off his head.

"Just wanted to see if you were solid."

"I'd like to point out that you're suffering from heatstroke and talking to a dead man," Renny said, picking up the finger bone from where it had dropped. "My solidity may be part of your hallucination. And hallucination or not, don't think I missed how you didn't answer my question. Why," he pressed, pointing the finger bone at Gideon, "did you decide to take the walk?"

Gideon eyed the bone before meeting Renny's expectant gaze. "I could ask you the same thing."

Renny let the bony projectile drop to join its fellows. "I suppose you could."

CHAPTER 16
DAY 861

A LITTLE OVER A YEAR AFTER HE RETURNED RENNY'S shard, Gideon, Doc, Kneecaps, Renny, Nyal, and a new inmate named Joss were in the middle of a game of net the queen.

There had been some worry over Renny and Gideon playing on opposite teams, but Renny's campaign had, to Gideon's mind, become more habit than obsession, and both promised, on pain of sacrificing half their morning rations, that they would behave.

Even that might not have been enough to soothe Doc's concerns, but Renny had also allowed Kneecaps to keep possession of his beloved shard for the duration of the game.

Secure that the Morton rules of no killing or unnecessary maiming were in force, the game commenced without incident until the third quarter.

Gideon had just saved the queen—a non-regulation lump of pineapple leather filled with grit and sutured together by Doc— from a foul to left field when Nyal's alarmed "*Uh-oh*" rose from the end zone, where the youngest inmate was serving as Keeper.

Looking past Nyal's shoulder, Gideon immediately spied what had caused the comment.

"Looks like Pavel's lost his temper," Kneecaps observed from her spot as scout.

"Must be a day of the week," Renny said as Gideon moved closer to see Pavel's ire fixed on a grifter who'd arrived on the last transport 'ship. Gideon thought the guy's name was Harry . . . or maybe Horace.

Could be Havarti.

Anyway, rumor had it he was in for having run a con on the wrong risto.

At the moment, Pavel was hauling Harry-Horace-Havarti up by the collar, so his toes barely scraped the red grit of the yard.

Harry-Horace-Havarti was raising his hands, palms out in the universal gesture of "Please don't kill me, but if you have to kill me, please don't let it hurt." His expression was a perfect blend of panic, appeasement, and innocence.

Probably the panic and appeasement were real.

Innocence, as Gideon well knew, had relative degrees in the Barrens. But as Harry-Horace—*Horatio*, that was it!—Horatio didn't look like a complete idiot, Gideon also doubted the young man had done anything to deliberately set Pavel off. It was just that Pavel was the living analogue of a flawed crystal . . . one wrong move and—*boom*.

With a resigned sigh, Gideon tossed the queen over to Doc, who nabbed it in a neat underhand, and set off towards the homicide in progress.

"I'll set up a cot for you then, shall I?" Doc asked as Gideon passed.

"A little faith?" Gideon hefted his stick as he turned to walk backwards, facing Doc and the rest of the players as he moved towards Pavel and Horatio.

"I got two smokes says Pavel at least cracks a rib," Kneecaps offered, coming up alongside Doc.

"I'll take that," Joss said in their soft Macintosh dialect while, from behind them, Renny loomed with his own stick in hand.

"Try not to let Pavel kill you," he called out to Gideon. "That's my—"

"—job," Gideon cut in as he came within range of his target. "Thanks. I got the brief."

As he spoke, he spun on one heel to swing his queen stick between Pavel's fist and Horatio's panic-stricken face.

The crack of Pavel's knuckles to the stick was prodigious, and Gideon felt the impact all the way to his shoulders.

"Damn it to Earth and back," Pavel swore, dropping Horatio and shaking his sore knuckles. "Why are you being so crazy?"

"It's a calling," Gideon said as he swung the stick up to rest on his shoulder. "So, what's the buzz?"

"I should be asking that," Pavel groused, kissing his knuckles while reaching over to grab a quietly retreating Horatio with his free hand. "You interrupt my teaching this wasp a lesson."

"Oh?" Gideon looked at Horatio, whose lips were moving quickly in what Gideon recognized as the mantra for inner peace. "What kind of lesson?"

"I teach him not to be looking at me funny."

Gideon turned to Horatio. "Did you look at him funny?"

"I don't even know what the bloke means," Horatio replied, his lower Nikean dialect thick as mortar.

Pavel gave him a shake. "You saying you did not look at me?"

"No!" Horatio's hands rose again. "I was just looking your way, right? And you was looking my way, and you know, then we was looking at each other, like."

Gideon squelched the sigh. Pavel had many skills, but reading facial expressions wasn't one of them.

"You *smiled*," Pavel growled the word.

"Just bein' friendly, mate."

"We are not mates." Pavel hauled Horatio close. "We are not even dating."

"No, not like that," Horatio protested.

"Why?" Pavel gave him a little shake. "You would not want to be dating me?"

"Mind if I help out?" Gideon asked, before things devolved further.

Horatio's deep brown eyes shot his way. "Oh, please."

"So, Pavel," Gideon began. "I'm sure Horus—"

"*Horatio . . .*" Horatio hissed, looking ashen.

"Horatio," Gideon corrected himself, "didn't mean to offend."

"How would you be knowing this?" Pavel asked, lowering Horatio a fraction, enough for his toes to touch the ground.

"Because we met on the Outside."

"You have?" Pavel asked.

"We have?" Horatio murmured.

"Sure," Gideon said, sending Horatio a look that said *stop talking now.*

Luckily for Horatio, he was better at reading facial expressions than Pavel, because his mouth snapped shut so fast, Gideon heard his teeth clack.

Satisfied, Gideon looked at Pavel. "We crossed paths back in the day," he explained. "We were both working the same street in Nike. I caught Har-Horatio, here trying to pull a two-finger dip on one of my marks."

"I thought you were being a soldier, back in the day," Pavel said, his heavy brow furrowing.

"Sure," Gideon agreed, "but a guy's gotta keep a hand in. Anyway, I warned Horatio off, and he showed the appropriate professional courtesy and moved on."

"So you are not friends," Pavel said.

"No," Gideon said, and as Horatio's expression fell, added, "we're more than friends. We're family—all part of the clan of thieves, grifters, dippers, killers, and cons. He's one of us," Gideon said, fixing his gaze on Pavel. "And being as he *is* one of us, maybe you could see your way to giving him another chance?"

For a moment, he watched Pavel's face working through the philosophical implications of Gideon's statement.

At last, Pavel's eyes cleared and flicked from Horatio to Gideon. "I think this is true, about all of us being family," he said.

"Bloomin' marvelous," Horatio began.

"But," Pavel cut him off with a glare. "Even family has a hierarchy, yes?"

It took a few seconds for Gideon to get past hearing the word "hierarchy" coming out of Pavel's mouth to respond, "I guess so?"

"And in the Barrens' hierarchy," Pavel continued, "I would be the Papa. Only, some of the little brothers are looking to be the new Papa," Pavel said, sending a glance over the yard, now filled with watching eyes. "So if they think Papa is being soft, they might start to make life hard for him. And *he* is *me*," he added, in case Gideon was having trouble keeping up.

"So you can't afford to look soft," Gideon said, because it was, in fact, far too easy to keep up.

"Exactly," Pavel beamed, then frowned, because smiling would, no doubt, contribute to the perception of his going soft. "So in order to hold on to my place in hierarchy, I can either continue to teach the little man a lesson—"

"*I'm five-ten,*" Horatio muttered.

"Or I can teach the man who interrupted the lesson a lesson," Pavel continued, looking from Horatio to Gideon and back.

"Either way, you're looking at solitary," Gideon pointed out.

"I do many days alone," Pavel said. "It is good meditation time. Plus, I keep my place at the head of the family."

Gideon considered Horatio, who was looking like a man resigned to death, then at Pavel, then lifted the stick from where it rested on his shoulder. "Okay," he said, "I'll do you both a solid, but try not to break anything important."

"Wait," Horatio said, waving his hands. "You can't—I can't let you get beat up for me," he protested, his dialect suddenly sounding a lot less Nike gutter.

"Sure you can," Gideon said, easing back and gripping the stick with both hands. "For old times' sake."

"But . . ." Horatio began, then let out a whoop as Pavel flung him aside.

"Quinn!" Pavel roared, squaring off with Gideon. "You cause me trouble for last time!" And then he dove straight at Gideon in a full-body tackle.

Gideon, though he'd prepared himself for the attack, soon discovered there was no preparation great enough to withstand the shock of a charging Pavel.

He did get the stick moving, and even heard it thud against Pavel's shoulder, right before his ears were filled with the *whoosh* of air escaping his lungs as Pavel drove him to the ground.

He felt, more than heard, the crack of a rib under the giant's weight.

Pain, and a redness that had nothing to do with the rising puffs of dust, filled his eyes, while he heard, as if from very far away, the sound of the COs' whistles and authoritative shouts.

He also caught a distant *"Tokk"* in Pavel's Stoli accent, and then a thick Nikean "Thanks, mate."

That last was followed by a distinctly Adian, "There'll be a reckoning for this."

Distantly, Gideon wondered when Renny had joined the party, and what the swarm he meant by that.

He wanted to ask, but he was still having trouble making air move in and out of his lungs in a proper fashion.

Later, while Doc wrapped his ribs, Gideon explained the details leading to his, once again, taking up space in the infirmary. "Really, it could have gone worse," he concluded, after describing Pavel's reasoning.

"No doubt," Doc replied, fastening the bandage around Gideon's cracked ribs. "Kneecaps says thank you for the cigarettes, by the way."

"Hey, at least my negotiating skills are improving," Gideon offered.

Doc held out a cup of water and two anti-inflammatories. "You could write a book."

CHAPTER 17
DAY 865

Cracked rib notwithstanding, Gideon was back in the veins only a few days after the Horatio incident.

Since Pavel had actually held back some—after all, the rib was cracked, not broken—Gideon knew he should count himself lucky.

But even as he dug his spade deeper into the earth around the hunk of crystal-rich shard he'd chosen, he didn't feel lucky.

More than anything, he felt wary.

Admittedly, that wariness could be due to his current work-site—a deep crevice in the desert floor that measured a crooked fifteen meters long, and only three meters at its widest point.

Gideon tried to view the claustrophobic location as a blessing.

If nothing else, it spared him the caustic glares Renny had been throwing his way since the day Gideon stepped between Pavel's fist and Horatio's face.

Unfortunately, a lack of vindictive Renny did little to ease his nerves, which continued to stretch until he felt certain he could count the fingers of tension dancing up his spine.

He was so wired, in fact, that on hearing a spatter of gravel from behind, he sprung to his feet and hauled the spade up to defend himself against all comers.

A quick scan of the rock face revealed the source of the disturbance to be a common scarab, climbing up the side of the gorge, its horns shifting in a steady rhythm as it went.

Gideon grimaced at his own skittishness, then sneered at the bug, which ignored him.

"Be that way," Gideon huffed at the indifferent scarab, and turned back to his excavation, but before he could slide the spade into the dirt, three long whistles, followed by three short, sounded the warning of an unstable vein.

Following protocols drilled in from his first days in the Barrens, he grabbed his spade and his crystal canister and headed for the path that led out of the defile.

His first priority was to get away from the vein.

His second was to render any assistance, should it be needed.

He hoped assistance would be needed, as the alternative meant there wasn't enough left of whomever had triggered the event *to* assist.

Preoccupied by the mental review of triage procedures, Gideon didn't see the shadow that fell across his upward path.

At least, he didn't see it until said shadow's foot was shooting into his chest, sending him tumbling back to the rocky floor of the gorge, canister falling one way, spade another.

The fall knocked out whatever air the kick had left in him, so for a moment all Gideon knew was the shriek of his ribs and the wheeze of his lungs as he tried to inhale.

His brain said *ouch.*

His body shuddered.

His mind tumbled, much like the barrage of pebbles dancing down the slope.

But as a fresh round of whistles filtered through the pain,

Gideon sucked in a dusty lungful of air and rolled to one side . . . only to be kicked back.

"Not this time," he heard someone say.

Gideon squinted into the red to see the shadow resolve itself into Renny, who said, in a voice dripping with disdain, "This time Gideon Quinn will not be rushing to the rescue like the hero from one of your quarterstar dreadfuls." As he spoke, crystal-light bounced off the shard in Renny's right hand, while the fallen spade, in his left, pressed down on Gideon's chest.

"Smog it," Gideon spat, but he didn't try to move, not with the sharp edge of the spade digging through his shirt. "What did you do?"

"Nothing fatal," Renny said. "Yet." Then he lifted the spade. Probably, Gideon thought, with the intention of driving it straight through Gideon's chest.

Not wanting to confirm the theory, Gideon rolled quickly to his left. So quickly, in fact, the blade hadn't even cleared all the way, leaving him with a slice across his chest to add its own queasy harmony to the chorus of injuries.

Renny cursed and adjusted his aim, targeting Gideon's head.

Gideon responded by rolling forward, rib protesting the entire way.

He only made it to his knees when he heard the reverberant *clang* of the spade head striking the wall of the gorge.

The noise of that impact had both Gideon and Renny freezing and casting a wary eye at the nearby vein, which, thankfully, continued to *not* explode.

That half a breath of wariness allowed Gideon time to scramble to his feet and throw a kick, just as Renny was turning back to the fray.

It wasn't much of a kick, but it did catch Renny in the side, forcing him to drop the spade, which Gideon reclaimed as Renny staggered back.

"Damn you," Renny hissed, recovering. "Damn you to Earth and back."

"Right back at you," Gideon hissed before leaping back from a sudden feint. "Do you really want to die here?" he asked, swiping at Renny.

"Not particularly," Renny replied. "But if that's what it takes to end you, I'll happily go to my forest."

"That's how you want it? Great," Gideon said. "But before they plant our trees, will you—*please*—tell me what on smogging Earth I ever did to you?"

"What you did?" Renny echoed as, to Gideon's shock, his expression suddenly shattered. "What you did," he said again, "was to not *once* be able to remember what it was you did."

CHAPTER 18
BACK IN THE DAY

Fort Echo - Northern Adian Territories
December 3, 1441 After Landing

"I said, who goes there?"

As Gideon watched, the shadow who'd spoken stepped cautiously away from the open door of the gatehouse.

Showtime, Gideon thought. "Major Carillon and company out of the Fourth Legion," Gideon called back in a long-practiced Adian accent

Even as he spoke, the figure paused, and Gideon noted the moment the sentry spied two columns of infantry emerging from the curtain of rain behind him.

There followed a lengthy pause, and Gideon wondered if, by some obscene chance, the Adian soldier was acquainted with Carillon.

At his left, Fehr's hand shifted on his sword's hilt while, behind him, Gideon was certain Nbo had her crossbow to hand.

Then the figure seemed to relax. "Advance and be recognized!" he called back.

"*Finally*," Gideon muttered before following the prompt.

As he neared the gatehouse, the shadow of a sentry resolved into a tall figure, swathed in the same hooded cloak Gideon's company wore.

In tonight's weather, the guard's hood was raised, so all Gideon could make out was the tip of a nose and the flash of a rank tab identifying him as a sergeant.

Gideon tugged at his own dripping cloak, but left his hood down. He wanted the guard to see his face. That seeming-transparency was meant to assure any Adians he met that Gideon was exactly who he said he was, and therefore to be trusted.

The strategy paid off, as the sergeant lowered his weapon and offered a crisp salute—slapping the blade of his hand to his head in the Eastern fashion. "Major Carillon," he said, dropping the hand back to his side. "Welcome to Fort Echo," he added, with a quick glance back at the gatehouse.

"Thank you, Sergeant . . .?" Gideon paused expectantly.

"Butcher," the man replied, before turning back to face Gideon. "Sergeant Clarence Butcher, at your service, sir." Though even as he made the promise, his attention again drifted towards the open door of his shelter.

This time Gideon followed the glance, but saw only a pair of oiled canvas bags, similar to those he'd seen being loaded onto the *Bounty*. "Did we interrupt your tea?" he asked Butcher with what he felt was an appropriate level of sarcasm.

"*No, sir!*" The sergeant aimed his hood back in Gideon's direction with a snap. "Would you like me to radio the duty officer, Major?"

"No time for that," Gideon said, jerking his chin at Eitan, who stepped forward at the cue. "My radio operator intercepted a mission brief for a Colonial company we believe to be operating behind the lines. According to the message, this company has orders to destroy the ARAS *Bounty*. Tonight."

"Sabotage an airship? And over a hundred kilometers behind the lines?" Butcher scoffed. "That's smogged."

At Gideon's left, Eitan cleared his throat. Loudly enough Butcher couldn't help but hear.

"That's smogged, *sir*," Butcher corrected himself.

"No one ever accused the Colonials of good sense," Gideon said as Eitan, continuing to play his part, held a folded sheet of weather-treated parchment out to the sergeant.

"This is the transmission we intercepted," Gideon explained.

The sergeant automatically reached out to accept the parchment, brushing Eitan's fingers. The contact caused Butcher to start and almost drop the message.

Gideon suppressed a sigh.

During his short time serving with Eitan Fehr, Gideon had become accustomed to the Fujian sensitive's effect on people.

While the sergeant mumbled an apology and bent over the parchment, Eitan turned away, allowing Gideon one quick view of the distaste in his expression before Butcher looked up.

"These orders are for the Colonial Twelfth," the sergeant said, waving the parchment. "*Quinn's* Dirty Dozen."

"You've heard of Quinn?" Gideon asked, not bothering to hide his surprise.

"Everyone's heard of Quinn," Butcher replied.

"Really?" Gideon asked, glancing back at Nbo. He couldn't see under the hood, but he was pretty sure she was rolling her eyes.

"Word has it that Quinn himself murdered a Midasian of rank in the heart of the Ducati fort, a couple years back," Butcher mused, still studying the message.

"Yes," Gideon said, though his throat felt suddenly tight.

"Quinn is a very bad man. One who, according to those orders in your hand, is planning to destroy the *Bounty* tonight, at twenty-eight hundred hours."

"It's coming up on twenty-eight hundred hours now," Butcher observed, his hood swiveling once again towards the gatehouse.

"That it is," Gideon agreed. Waited a beat. "Don't you think we should stop him?"

"Sir! Yes, sir," the other man agreed, snapping another of those concussive salutes. "Let me just get the gate for you," Butcher said, spinning on one heel and splashing to the portcullis control with surprising alacrity.

"That was unexpected," Eitan murmured.

"*Not now*," Gideon hissed, though he was as surprised as the lieutenant at Butcher's eagerness.

Truth was, he'd been expecting a little more resistance—at least an offer to radio the fort's commanding officer—before opening the gate and inviting a strange company inside.

"The *Bounty* is mid-field," Butcher called over his shoulder as he hauled on the lever that activated the portcullis. As the gate groaned its way up, he let out a steaming puff of breath and turned to face Gideon. "There are six guards, three aboard the *Bounty*, three patrolling. Lieutenant Anapopoulis is in command and will assist as needed."

"*Wow*," Gideon said under his breath, then shared a look with Eitan, who shrugged.

"Ready when you are, Major," Butcher continued, locking the gate open.

Still, Gideon hesitated. Surely it couldn't be this easy.

Could it?

Then again, he reminded himself, if anything were truly amiss, Eitan would have caught it during his brief contact with Butcher.

With a huff of acceptance that steamed the air in front of him, Gideon gestured his people forward, then waited with Eitan on the opposite side of the gate from Butcher.

Once Walsie and Hamish—again humming his favorite tune—splashed past, Gideon and Eitan fell in behind. But after only a few steps, Gideon turned back to the gate, which was already lowering.

"Butcher?" he called out, but rain and the gate must have made it tough for the sergeant to hear, so he tried again. "*Butcher!*" When *that* failed to get the man's attention, he tried another tack. "*Clarence!*"

"Sir!" Butcher straightened and peered through the lowering cross-hatch of the portcullis.

"Thanks for the assist!" Gideon told him. "I'll be sure to make note of it in my report."

"Very decent of you, sir!" Butcher called back, just as a gust of wind flipped Butcher's hood back, giving Gideon a brief flash of pale skin and the whip of long black hair.

Then the gate squished to the ground and Butcher flipped his hood back in place.

"So far, so good," Gideon said as the trio neared the *Bounty*, hovering placidly at anchor. A glance had Walsie, Hamish, and the rest of the company peeling off to deal with the three perimeter guards Butcher had mentioned.

"It would have been easier to kill the sentry," Eitan pointed out.

"Easier," Gideon agreed, "but if anyone came along and found the body, it'd put a wasp in the whole plan."

"There'll be seven hells to pay when the Coal-fart brass learns he let us through. I almost feel sorry for the guy," Nbo added, pulling her crysto-plas rifle from under her cloak.

"Do not waste your pity on that one," Eitan said, drawing his sword.

"You sensed something?" Nbo asked, looking past Gideon at the sensitive.

"Something. Yes," Eitan said, but didn't elaborate, and since they'd reached the gangplank, Gideon had no time to ask what he meant.

From here on in, all his thoughts were on getting the *Bounty* out of the hands of the Adians and into the supply sheds of the Colonial quartermasters.

CHAPTER 19
DAY 865

"The *Bounty*," Gideon said, his vision clearing, just in time to bat another feint from Renny's shard to one side.

"Yes," Renny agreed, his teeth bared. "The *Bounty*."

"You were the guard at Fort Echo?" Gideon asked.

"Of *course* I was the smogging guard!" Renny shouted.

"No. That can't be." Gideon frowned.

"Why ever not?"

"That guy's name was Butcher."

"Butcher?" Renny said, so shocked he actually lowered the shard. "Are you deaf as well as blind?"

"I'm just telling you what I heard," Gideon said.

"I very clearly said my name was Boucher."

"Well, it was raining pretty hard," Gideon allowed. "But what about the Clarence? Oh," he said, even as Renny's lips curled, "never mind. Clarence . . . Renny. I get it."

"Give the man a gold rubik," Renny said.

"So you were the sergeant on the gate?"

"I was the sergeant whose life you ruined, and then promptly forgot," Renny corrected.

"I didn't forget you," Gideon pointed out. "I remembered

Clarence Butcher just fine. Maybe if you hadn't been wearing one of those Adian 'hide from the world' hoods, I would have put the two of you together."

"It was raining," Renny pointed back. "Everyone was wearing their hood, except you . . . and your beautiful second." Gideon watched Renny's eyes warm as he mentioned Eitan. "I often wondered what happened to him."

"He's on the wall of my cell," Gideon said flatly.

"A pity," Renny said. "But I suppose that's what happens to people you touch. They die, or they're ruined, so they might as well be dead."

"I'd like to point out you're not dead," Gideon said.

"Always an answer." Renny murmured. "You may have left me alive, that night," he continued, flipping the dagger back to his right hand, "but your actions did cause a death. Two, in fact."

CHAPTER 20
BACK IN THE DAY

Fort Echo - Northern Adian Territories
December 3, 1441 After Landing

In the sheeting rain outside Fort Echo, Clarence waited for the portcullis to close behind Major Carillon, then returned to the gatehouse.

Pax Van Meer, a shadow trader with whom he had a longstanding relationship, was due any minute.

As he crouched in the gatehouse, double-checking the fastenings on the oiled canvas bags, he hoped Pax hadn't been scared off by Carillon's company.

All in all, it would be best if he were quit of the stolen weapons before he radioed in the major's arrival, *and* the potential attack by the infamous Colonel Quinn.

And when he *did* raise the alarm? Who knew, but he might even net a medal for his part in preventing the loss of the *Bounty.*

Possibly even a promotion.

Looking up from the bags, he caught sight of another light

crisscrossing the icy plains and immediately dismissed thoughts of advancement.

Slinging his crysto-plas rifle over his chest, Clarence grabbed the two heavy sacks and stepped out into the rain to complete the night's business.

"It's about time," he said, hauling the bags in the direction of the light. "Oy!" he complained as the light swept up, temporarily blinding him. "Watch where you're aiming that, Pax."

"Who is Pax?" an authoritative voice boomed through the drumming rain.

Clarence stifled the curse. "Ahh, General Vern?" Affecting a confused tone, he let one duffel splat to the wet ground while he clutched the other in front of the rifle. "What are you doing out in this weather?"

"One of the exploring teams reported enemy movement within a kilometer of the fort. Who is Pax?" she asked again. "And what are you doing with those duffels?"

"Oh," Clarence said with a smile the general couldn't see. "That's just the nickname I've given Master Sergeant Gifford. Because he's always telling people to give him some peace, so—pax—peace. Get it?"

"That's a terrible nickname," Vern determined. "And the bags?"

"Extra rain kit," Renny said quickly.

The general's aide, a strapping young corporal named Tzitzin, aimed his torch to the bag on the ground.

"About those enemy movements," Clarence said before Tzitzin's light revealed anything, "I was just about to radio in that I've received confirmation of an active threat against the fort and the *Bounty*."

"And how would you know that?" The question came not

from Vern, but from Tzitzin, which Clarence thought a bit cheeky.

"Boucher?" Vern prompted. "Answer the question."

"Sir," Clarence said, then took a breath. "Several minutes ago, I was approached by Major Carillon's company, out of the Fourth Legion. They've intercepted a radio transmission between Colonial Epsilon Command and the Twelfth Company."

"Quinn's Dirty Dozen," Vern murmured, her breath wisping through the sleet.

"The very same." Renny nodded. "I have the transmission from Carillon's second himself." As he spoke, he dug the paper he'd received from his pocket. "As you will read, Quinn has orders to destroy the ARAS Bounty tonight."

"That's impossible," Vern stated flatly, and Renny, holding the message outstretched, felt the hot spike of anger running up his spine at her off-handed rejection of the facts.

"Quinn's a madman," Tzitzin offered, "but coming this deep into enemy territory is off the apiary, even for him."

"Not that part." Vern drew her night-vision spyglass and raised it towards the sleeting skies. "The bit about Carillon."

Clarence frowned. "What about—?"

"Tzitzin!" Vern's snap interrupted his query. "Radio the duty officer to sound the alarm."

"Yes, sir!"

"What?" Renny asked, while the eager Tzitzin unhooked his radio.

Vern lowered the spyglass. "Tell me, Sergeant, do you hear anything?"

Clarence began to protest there was nothing to hear but the never-ending rain, but then he caught the sound, faint at first, of an airship's engines, their thrum almost masked by the storm.

Even as he identified the sound of engines, the general alarm shrieked through the fort, waking the legion.

Renny sensed a change in the light and, looking up, spied the long, bulbous shadow climbing fast as it angled towards the northwest.

Several flashes of plasma shot skyward, to no avail. The airship was already out of range.

"I don't understand," Clarence said, though he did. Of course he did.

"I do," Vern said. "Because today's dispatches included the report that Major Carillon was wounded in action three days ago, when he and his company were attacked by marauders, who successfully made away with the company's supplies. Including their uniforms."

"But if Carillon is WIA," Tzitzin asked, as if playing the puppy-eyed assistant in some detective pastiche, "who just flew away in the *Bounty*?"

"I imagine that would have been Gideon Quinn," Vern said, then glanced at Clarence. "Wouldn't you?"

Clarence, however, was already working the numbers.

On the minus side, allowing himself to be duped by an enemy was bad.

On the plus side, Quinn had obviously gotten past Lieutenant Anapopoulis, *and* a minimum of five other members of the legion to get aboard the 'ship, which meant Clarence wasn't the only smog-up in the mix.

On the minus side, and it was a big minus, he was standing in front of his commanding officer in possession of two sacks crammed to bursting with stolen weapons.

"Sergeant Boucher seems to have lost his voice," Vern said, turning to Tzitzin. "Corporal," she began. "Please remove the sergeant's—"

But whatever order she was about to give her aide was never delivered, because the general was suddenly preoccupied by the smoke emerging from the plasma bolt Clarence had just fired into her chest.

"Sorry, Tzitzin," Clarence said, aiming his rifle at the corporal. "The numbers just didn't work in your favor."

CHAPTER 21
DAY 865

GIDEON'S BREATH HUFFED OUT AS THE ARROW OF RENNY'S explanation struck home, then again, as Renny's blade swept in.

Metal spade clanged dully against stone dagger, and then both men leapt back to reset.

"You're saying you murdered your commanding officer?" Gideon asked in a pained breath.

"What choice did I have?" Renny asked, the shard weaving in front of him. "What choice did you leave me?"

"You had the advantage of surprise," Gideon almost spat with exasperation. "You could have disabled them, taken their radios, and made your escape."

"And what makes you think it could ever be that easy?"

"Because I've *done* it," Gideon replied. "A lot."

"Of course you have," Renny snarled. "Because you're nothing but a thief."

"So are you," Gideon pointed out. "I'm just better at it."

Renny's response to that was less wordy and more stabby, and Gideon was hard pressed to defend against the series of feints and jabs before he got a good slice to Renny's shin, sending the Adian limping in reverse.

"There's only one thing I don't understand," Gideon admitted as Renny dug in, blood and sweat dripping.

"And what is that?" Renny asked, delivering another broad slash.

"Why today?" Gideon dodged the first swipe, parried the second, shoved Renny away.

"What do you mean?" Renny pushed off the wall of the defile.

"I mean," Gideon said between gasps for breath, "for over two years you've been taking jabs at me, but you've never been this . . . rabid," he decided. "Why are you so smogging mad now?"

"I am so *smogging mad*," Renny said with clear disgust, "because you remembered *him*."

"What?" Gideon asked, straightening. "I mean, *who*?"

"*Horatio*," Renny hissed the name. "A grifter. A nobody. A piece of trash you passed on the street . . . once. And yet, years later, he shows up in the Barrens, and you remember every detail of that moment."

"Ah," Gideon said. "Well, I—"

"You took *everything* from me!" Renny cut in, spit flying as he threw his arms out wide. "Everything! And for over two years, I have been in your face, dropping hints the size of mammoth turds as to where you went wrong, but not once—not once—could you remember me, or where or how we'd met."

"I can see how that would be upsetting," Gideon agreed while, on the ground behind Renny, he caught a shimmer that did not come from the crystal bed.

"Upsetting?" Renny echoed, the anger in his expression shifting to the more familiar murderous. "Did anyone ever tell you that you've an annoying ability to understate the matter?"

"It's a gift," Gideon agreed, his glance flicking from Renny's shard to the shimmer and back.

"Allow me to give you another," Renny said, hefting his shard.

"Okay, but do you mind ducking first?" Gideon asked.

Without waiting for a reply, he spun the spade in an overhead arc, aiming directly for Renny's skull.

Lucky for his head, Renny *did* duck, slicing at Gideon at the same time.

Gideon felt the sick tearing of the shard parting flesh even as he altered his angle of attack, driving the spade, not into any of Renny's parts, but straight down and into the ground, where it bisected the viper that had been about to bury its fangs in Renny's leg.

At his side he heard an intake of breath, looked over his shoulder to see Renny spinning to stare at the two halves of a viper twitching their last.

Renny swore, then spun again to glare at Gideon. *"Why?"*

Gideon's mouth opened, though he had no idea what he meant to say, and anyway, by that point he was starting to notice the bleeding, which was becoming insistent.

Looking down, he saw a thick dark stain spreading over the sweat-stained gray of his shirt. "Oh," he said, and then felt his knees give way. "I think that's where you got me the first time," he added, pressing his hand over the wound.

"Answer the question," Renny demanded, as if Gideon hadn't spoken.

Gideon looked up to see Renny kneeling in front of him. "I guess I don't want you dead."

And while he didn't know what reaction he expected, it certainly wasn't to see the ice storm of Renny's hatred melting into a pale and wretched grief.

"You should," Renny said, his head weaving back and forth, much as the viper's had, just before Gideon killed it. "You *should* want me dead."

"Probably," Gideon admitted.

"But you don't."

"No."

"Why?" Renny asked again.

"Because I lied," Gideon said, his head tilting as he eyed Renny's face, which seemed suddenly to be framed by shadows.

"You'll have to be more specific."

"About Horatio," Gideon clarified.

"I don't understand."

"I lied about knowing Horatio," Gideon explained through teeth clenched against all manner of pains. "I never laid eyes on the guy before he stepped off the airship, last week."

"You *pretended* to know him?" Renny's expression blanked. "Why would you do that?"

Gideon shrugged, but the pain of that motion had the darkness around Renny's face shuddering and sending out blobs of black. "Classic de-escalation," he said, while the spade he'd forgotten he held dropped from numb fingers to thud to the ground. "Learned it from my fagin. Someone's in trouble, you make sure the trouble sees them as human. Better chance of survival. Pavel had to see Horatio as one of us, so I made him one of us."

"One of us," Renny echoed, glaring at Gideon.

Idly, Gideon wondered if Renny planned going for the throat or the heart.

He hoped he didn't aim for the gut.

Gut wounds were the worst.

Then, much to Gideon's surprise, Renny took him by the shoulders and helped ease him the rest of the way to the ground.

"I'll send someone," Renny said, then shoved himself to his feet, turned away, and strode out of Gideon's shrinking range of vision.

Why? The well-worn question wafted through Gideon's

thoughts, a brief flicker of light as the dark finally closed over his eyes.

It wasn't until he woke in the infirmary—again—that Gideon learned Renny had indeed sent help.

And while the CO's were sorting out how to get Gideon back to the prison, Renny had turned on his heel and walked away.

And kept walking.

"Why?" Gideon asked, out loud this time, but to that Doc had no answer.

CHAPTER 22
DAY 1561

Leaning against a shelf of rock, Gideon turned to look at Renny, resting comfortably on the other side of the skeleton. He had to squint, as the suns were setting behind the other man.

"So why didn't you do it?" he asked as Renny turned to meet his gaze. "You wanted me dead for years, but when you finally could have finished it, you walked away. All the way away," he said, indicating the surrounding desert. "Why?"

"Are you asking the ghost or the hallucination?" Renny asked in his turn.

Gideon grimaced. "Never mind."

"I rather think I have to," Renny said thoughtfully. "Very well." He gave himself a shake and shifted to face Gideon, his legs crossed in front of him. "I walked away because in that moment, the moment I could easily have stuck my shard in your gut—"

"You'd have gone for the gut?" Gideon cut in.

"I wanted you to suffer," Renny reminded him.

"Well, yeah, but there's suffering and *suffering*."

"Do you want to hear this or not?"

"Sorry." Gideon waved at him to continue.

"The simple fact is," Renny said, "as I looked at you, envisioning your demise, I was also struck by the realization of what waited beyond your death."

"And that would be?"

"Nothing." Renny held Gideon's gaze as he went on. "With a life sentence, and no more Gideon Quinn to hate, all that remained was year after year of . . . nothing. No more revenge to plan, no more battles to fight. I'd made despising you my reason. Once you were gone, I'd have been left with nothing. It was then I decided it would be better to die with *something*—even if that something was a bone-deep hatred—than continue to respirate, empty of anything resembling purpose."

The explanation complete, he studied Gideon. "Well?"

"Well, what?" Gideon asked.

"I've shown you mine. Don't you wish to similarly unburden yourself?"

"Not so much," Gideon decided, leaning back against the rock wall and closing his eyes—only to open them again when he felt a ping of something hard glance off his head. "Hey!" He glared at Renny, who already had another finger bone flying from his hand. Gideon batted the second missile aside. "Stop it!"

"No." Renny picked up another piece of the unfortunate corpse. "I can keep this up forever. Or until you die. Either works, really."

"Keepers," Gideon hissed. "What will it take to make you go away?"

"The truth, I imagine," Renny said. "But since you're the one hallucinating me, you might ask yourself why you want me to know why you're here." He stopped. "I may have made myself dizzy."

"You're not the only one," Gideon huffed. "Anyway, why does it matter why I'm here?"

"I don't know," Renny admitted. "But it must, or else why would I also be here, asking?"

Gideon blinked, then rubbed his dry eyes. "This is a ridiculous argument," he decided.

"I couldn't agree more."

Gideon let his head fall back against the rock and, as Renny remained silent, let his mind drift.

With luck, it would drift all the way out of his body, and this farcical conversation would be over.

"I can't believe you're just giving up like this," Renny said, putting paid to that hope. "What would Nyal say?"

"Guess we'll never know," Gideon murmured to the back of his eyelids. "Seeing as he's gone."

CHAPTER 23
DAY 1002

"I've changed my mind. I'm not going."

Gideon, leaning in the open door of Nyal's cell, watched as the young man dropped the satchel containing his recently returned personals to the floor with a gentle *fwump*.

"I don't believe not going is an option," Doc said from where he sat on Nyal's cot, already stripped of its bedding. In his lap was a stack of books, pamphlets, and newspapers bequeathed to him by the newly paroled Nyal.

"It should be," Nyal insisted, spinning to face the medic. "I don't know what to do out there!"

"I do," Pavel said. He was looming at the rear of the cell, holding the replica of the Fujian Opera House Nyal had fashioned from bits of cardboard packing materials hoarded from the mess and infirmary. "What you must do, as soon as you get off the transport, is take a five-star from your allowance, go directly to Red Crystal Alley, and get your lance waxed."

Nyal shuddered. "Not my cuppa."

"I think Nyal's concerned more about the long term," Gideon said to Pavel.

"Oh." Pavel shrugged, carefully because of the opera house. "Maybe you could be robbing another bank?"

Nyal made a strangled noise and plopped down on the cot next to Doc.

"You know, you don't have to go back to Nike City," Doc said gently.

"But that's the thing," Nyal said. "It doesn't matter where I go, because anywhere I am, I will always have killed those guards."

"And you'll always have to carry that," Gideon said, shaking his head at Doc's warning glance. "But the fact you own up to that? Nyal—that's one of the main reasons you've been paroled."

"But no one asked me if I wanted to be paroled," Nyal snapped. "I'm telling you, I can't do it." He buried his head in his hands.

Now Gideon looked at Doc, but he apparently had no better idea than Gideon what to tell the young man.

"*Oi there!*"

Gideon turned to see Horatio jogging up the walkway to join him. He was slightly breathless, and holding a loose sheet of paper in his hand. Behind him, Kneecaps was trotting along as fast as her short legs would carry her.

"Gideon," Horatio nodded, then looked inside the cell. "Nyal!" He squeezed himself into the cramped space. "Keepers," he huffed, resting his hands on his knees. "I was that afraid I'd miss you."

"Actually . . ." Nyal began.

"Only, I just spied that model of the Santiago library you gave t'Kneecaps," he said, overriding the other man. "It's—smogging magnificent! It's the bees swarming knees! It's the bear dog's bollocks! Isn't that what I said?" he asked Kneecaps, who'd come puffing to a stop next to Gideon.

"He did," she gasped. "He said exactly that. It is a wonder,

Nyal," she said after heaving in a deep breath. "Thanks for leaving it with me."

"Oh." Nyal shrugged, still looking miserable. "It's nothing. Just a way to pass the time."

"Bollocks to that," Horatio waved him off. "Have you seen the thing?" he asked Doc, then continued before he could respond. "Our Nyal managed to build a replica, *to scale*, of the swarming Santiago Colonial Library—with a removable roof *and* detailed interior—out of nothing but playing cards and spent matches."

"Is that where my cards kept disappearing to?" Doc asked.

"Ha," Nyal said.

"If I was you, I'd be right chuffed," Horatio said to Nyal. Then his eyes latched onto the opera house in Pavel's hands. "*Keepers in the blooming comb*," he breathed, all admiration, and took a step forward.

"*Mine*," Pavel growled.

Horatio took a step back and turned back to Nyal. "What you have, mate," he said, his expression suddenly serious, "is a gift."

"It's just making things," Nyal said with a shrug. "The modeling's what got me into heists back in the day, when I was a thief," he added. In case, Gideon supposed, anyone in the prison cell had forgotten this. "It was all I ever knew, the thieving."

"Now you also know how to harvest crystal," Pavel pointed out.

"I hear it's a booming industry," Gideon said. "Sorry." He held up both hands as five pairs of eyes and an elbow from Kneecaps hit him. "Sometimes it's just too easy."

"At least here I have a place. And friends," Nyal said, looking up at the others.

"You have friends," Doc assured. "But there's no future for you here."

"There's no future for me out there either." Nyal gave the satchel a kick. "I don't even know anyone outside these walls. Not anymore."

"But that's why I came runnin' to find you before you scarped," Horatio told him. "Because I know *exactly* what you should do when you're back in the world."

"If it's anything to do with Red Crystal Alley, we've covered that one," Gideon told him.

"Never a bad option," Kneecaps admitted with a longing sigh.

"True," Horatio agreed. "But I was thinking more along the lines of this." He shoved the paper Gideon had noticed earlier into Nyal's hands. "Go to the Circus and ask after Divya," he said, pointing to a section of the paper that Gideon supposed was an address. "Even if she's not in town, the Circus folk will help you contact her. When you do, tell her I sent you. She'll give you a place to be," he promised, "and people to be with."

Nyal looked up from the sheet of paper. "Are you sure?" he asked, his eyes filled with a terrified hope as they latched on Horatio.

"Trust me," Horatio said, then winced. "But don't tell Divya I said that last bit. Just find her and show her what you can do with a matchbook and a set of playing cards. I promise, she'll find a place for you."

Nyal still looked uncertain.

"I believe you should listen to the little man," Pavel said.

"*Not that little,*" Horatio muttered.

"Nothing wrong with being little," Kneecaps added.

Pavel ignored the byplay. "You have a gift," he said to Nyal, nodding towards the opera house in his hands. "Maybe this Divya will help you use that gift. And," he continued thoughtfully, "if it turns out little man is lying about this Divya, you send me letter, and I will break him for you."

"Good talk." Gideon gave Horatio, who'd gone quite ashen, a bolstering pat on the shoulder.

Nyal stared at Pavel a moment, then turned to Horatio. "I'll do it," he said, tucking the paper in his shirt pocket. "And thanks."

"It'll be Divya and the Rogues thanking you," Horatio promised. "Especially if you can show her you know your way around a thrust."

"I thought we'd moved on from Red Crystal Alley," Gideon said, stepping aside in anticipation of Kneecap's pointed elbow.

CHAPTER 24
DAY 1561

"So, Nyal's not dead," Renny said as Gideon finished describing the safecracker's last day in Morton.

"Nope."

"You know, you could have led with that."

"Could have," Gideon agreed. "But this was more fun."

He didn't even complain when the next bony projectile bounced off his shoulder.

Renny heaved a prodigious sigh. "So who else made parole since I left?"

"Kneecaps got out last year," Gideon told him. "And Xi."

"Who?"

"Right." Gideon glanced over. "He didn't show up until after you . . ." Gideon waved at their surroundings. "Tzu Xi's a second-story man out of Epsilon. Took the eighteen months in Morton over five years in Guinness."

"Ah."

"Pavel got out too."

"*Seriously?*"

Gideon's lips quirked in understanding of Renny's shock.

"He was back in less than a month. Oh, and Kamal and Menk left," he said, thinking of the two guards. "Together."

Black-winged brows shot up. "You're joking."

"Not even a little. Put in their retirement papers and drafted the marriage agreement at the same time, right before flying off to join an agricenter near Kamal's hometown in Fuji."

"But . . . Kamal and *Menk?*"

"I guess it's true what they say about still waters," Gideon said.

"Well, yes. But there's still, and then there's stagnant," Renny pointed out.

Gideon choked on the laugh, then wondered how he could find anything funny just now.

Probably the delirium, he thought.

Then the delirium spoke again. "What about Cassandra?"

At the question, Gideon felt a chill that had nothing to do with the impending nightfall. "What about her?"

"Shouldn't she have been paroled by now, as well?"

"Should have," Gideon agreed, but couldn't quite bring himself to meet the dark gaze on the other side of the skeleton.

CHAPTER 25
DAY 1213

Squatting in the middle of his assigned vein, Gideon gently nestled the hunk of crystal he'd unearthed into a padded canister, then paused as a puff of dust tickled his nose.

With a grimace, he eased back on his heels and stared up at the bleached sky while, all around him, crystal hummed and picks scraped the hard, dry earth.

When the tickle faded, and no rogue sneeze threatened the stability of the canister, he closed and fastened the hinged lid and picked up his hard-won cargo.

Rising, he started down the long line of inmates, all hunkered over their own chosen clumps, as they counted down the baking minutes until the COs called time.

He angled away from the vein and towards the cargo mech, parked along with the personnel crawlers and rations cart, a safe distance from the vein.

Approaching the massed vehicles, huddled together with their wing-like solar shields spread wide, Gideon thought they looked like a nest of giant insects, napping in the suns until the time came to crawl back to the prison.

He was halfway to the caterpillar-treaded mechs when the

first sounds of trouble rose from the southwest curve of the vein; first in the form of shouts and curses, and followed by the dreaded six-toned whistle that signaled an unstable vein.

This last was followed by the equally dreaded shouts to "Clear! Clear! Clear!" and even as Gideon turned, the cylinder cradled in his arms, the previously somnolent desert erupted in a flood of motion.

All along the vein, prisoners and guards alike scrambled to get as far as possible from a potential explosion.

Gideon, already at a safe distance, remained still, staring towards the curve from which the disturbance had arisen.

He watched Horatio skitter past, and CO Woo slide up to assist a limping Mama to the relative safety of the transports.

Pavel came up short next to Gideon. "You should be moving," he said.

Gideon shifted the weight in his arms. "Why? What's happening?"

"Cassandra has gone swarm," Pavel said.

"Take this." Gideon shoved the canister at Pavel and took off running before he could think about what he was doing.

No one tried to stop him. Those who hadn't yet reached a safe distance were anxious enough to get there that they ignored his passage, and he soon came stumbling to a halt at the edge of a crop of mature crystals, well into the twinning stage.

Even in the current circumstances, he wondered at the sheer beauty of it all—the spires of crystal, their facets catching the sunlight and tossing it shimmering back to dance like stars over the dull red of the desert . . . and the woman standing in their midst.

"Cassandra," Gideon spoke her name softly as he came up alongside CO Kamal, who hadn't yet deserted the field.

A quick scan told Gideon why the guard remained—

Cassandra wasn't alone in the vein. At her feet, CO Menk lay unmoving, his close-cropped hair sticky with blood.

Gideon stepped forward, seeking a path between the clustered masses of crystal.

"*Quinn*," Kamal hissed the warning as he moved. "He's still alive."

Gideon's head dipped in acknowledgement of their warning, but he kept his eyes on Cassandra as he took another step.

Now he was close enough to hear her muttering to herself as her eyes danced from the crystal to Menk and back. Her hair, wild at the best of times, seemed to have come alive, dancing with static in the breathless air.

She held a pick, which swung wildly as she waved her arms, like one in the middle of a violent argument.

At her feet, Menk groaned. Her lips twisted. She raised the pick.

"Cassandra?" Gideon moved another step closer, hoping to draw her attention from the wounded man.

She froze, looked up. "Gideon?" she asked and then, as he watched, gave a whole body shudder, and the glassy-eyed anger cleared.

"Gideon," she said again, and for a moment he saw the woman who'd muscled her way into his cell, two years ago. "Fancy a cuppa?" Her smile beamed briefly before her brows furrowed in disapproval.

"Sure," he said. "Come on out and we'll get brewing."

"I would," she said with a toss of her head, "but you're still a feckin' idiot."

"Because I want to help you?"

"Because you think yourself a man of honor," she countered, pointing the pick in his direction. "Because you think anything you do will actually help. It won't," she said, letting the pick drop at her side. "In the end, you'll have saved no one."

Gideon froze.

"Oh! *Ohohoh!*" Cassandra said, putting a finger to her lips. "I forgot. I'm not supposed to tell."

"Tell what?" Kamal asked.

Cassandra looked at the guard, allowing Gideon to move another meter closer.

"That yon Gideon's innocent," she said so matter-of-factly that Gideon almost tripped and fell into a mass of crystal. "But he's wrong," she continued, clutching the pick in both hands. "There's no one innocent here. We're all of us wicked, all of us stained."

As she spoke, she raised the pick over her head in both hands.

Gideon cursed and was pretty sure he jumped the last half meter of distance, in time to intercept the pick before she could bring it down in the nearest clutch of crystal.

She snarled in his face, and held fast with a strength fed by madness as much as labor. Unable to wrench the tool from her hands, Gideon twisted the pick she held to one side, until both combatants were locked, side to side, by the weapon neither would release.

She was so close, Gideon could see the pulse fluttering at her throat.

Then she let out a sound, half laugh, half cry.

"I know you," she said, as if the last few moments had never happened.

Gideon, unnerved, met her gaze and found it to be clear. "I know you too," he began, only to be interrupted by a too-familiar *k-chunk.*

By the time the sound of the fired crossbow registered, Gideon was no longer fighting to prevent Cassandra from doing murder.

He was, instead, struggling to support her sagging body, from which the bolt fired by a late-arriving Tullaine quivered.

Cassandra's eyes remained open, locked on Gideon's as he, with the greatest care, lowered her so they both knelt in the vein's hollow, like the doomed lovers in one of Lonnie's theatricals.

Dying or not, Cassandra was what she was, and must have picked up his thought because her lips turned up, and she eased closer, so close he could feel the touch of her fluttering breath as she said, "And thus, with a kiss . . ."

"No," Gideon whispered, knowing the denial to be useless, for there was no more breath, no more light, no more life in the figure he held so close.

Later that evening, he was sitting on the edge of his bunk, stripped to the waist and staring at his damp shirt, which he'd draped over the back of the privy, when Doc appeared at the door of his cell.

"It's almost lockdown," Gideon told him without looking up.

"I know. But I thought you'd want to hear that I was able to meet with Warden Simkins."

Gideon met Doc's tired gaze. Waited.

"He says Menk will recover from his injuries."

"Okay."

"I was also, with CO Kamal's support, able to convince the warden that any inmates identifying as sensitives, of any strength or variety, should be kept out of the veins."

"Action without sufficient data?" Gideon asked bitterly, recalling Doc's refusal to pull Cassandra from the veins, two years past.

Doc grimaced and turned his eyes to the list carved into the wall behind Gideon. "As you pointed out some time ago, the Barrens are supposed to be a place of rehabilitation, not torture."

"That would be good, then," Gideon allowed.

"There was something else," Doc said.

Gideon waited.

"Kamal mentioned something about Cassandra saying you were innocent."

"She did," Gideon agreed, his voice neutral. "Right before she tried to spark a cache of crystal and blow us all back to Earth." He held the other man's gaze. "It was the madness talking."

"That's what Simkins said," Doc admitted.

Gideon nodded once before returning his attention to his damp shirt . . . and the bloodstains he hadn't been able to entirely wash out.

He heard Doc let out a huff of breath, and then the soft thud of his footsteps as he departed.

He was still sitting, staring at the dampened shirt, when CO Finch came by to lock his door for the night.

CHAPTER 26
DAY 1561

"Gideon . . . Gideon . . . *Gideonnnnnn . . .* Smog it, man, are you still with me?"

"Apparently," Gideon said, opening gummy eyes to find Tyche halfway sunk behind the Jackal's Fangs, staining the desert in shades of red that varied from Fujian Rose to battle-field bloody.

He wondered how long it had been since he'd told Renny what happened to Cassandra.

Then a terrible thought spiked through the haze. "Wait," he said as he sat up too quickly. "Wait," he said again, this time as he watched Renny divide into two, then slowly subside back into a single, annoying phantom. "Am I still alive?"

Renny let his eyes slide over the desert before sending Gideon a pointed look. "Why do you care?"

"I care," Gideon explained, "because if I were already dead, and you were still here, we could well be stuck together for a very long time."

"Oh," Renny said. "That would be . . ." he paused, seemingly at a loss.

"Excruciating," Gideon suggested.

Renny huffed. "No need to be cruel."

"Right, that's your thing."

"Was it cruel of me to leave you breathing, that day in the vein?"

"Maybe it was," Gideon said before he thought better.

"Oh?"

"No." Gideon clamped his mouth closed hard enough the teeth clacked. "I'm not getting into this. I have places to go and steps to count."

"Well then," Renny said as he popped to his feet, "let's be off, shall we?"

"There is no *we*," Gideon snarled.

"I beg to differ," Renny said.

Gideon's eyes closed, mostly to block the vision of Renny's smile. "What will it take to make you go away?"

For a time there was silence, and he dared hope the specter had fled. But when he opened his eyes, he found Renny was not only still present, he was crouched directly in front of him.

"Tell me why you're here," Renny said simply.

"Why?" Gideon asked, his voice cracking with more than thirst. "Why does it matter to you that I'm here?"

"I don't know," Renny admitted, his head tilting as he considered Gideon. "But it must, or I wouldn't keep asking, would I?"

At that question, Gideon's anger—and the strength that came with it—slid from his limbs and into the ground.

Sagging back against the rock, he let his arms rest on raised knees. "It's not that exciting," he warned.

"I'll be the judge of that."

"I guess you will." Gideon shook his head, but nothing, not even a snarky not-a-ghost, could shake free the failure that hovered over him like an Earth-born smog. "I was reading a newspaper," he began, and turned away from the expression of satisfaction on Renny's face.

CHAPTER 27
DAY 1560 - 1561

Replete with a dinner that had included the weekly fruit allowance, featuring a cup of chilled mango and blueberries, Gideon settled down in the yard with Doc and Horatio to read a three-month-old copy of the *Nike Daily News*.

Horatio was pouring over the entertainment section while Doc perused the colonial pages and Gideon devoured Nike's local reports with as much fervor as he would a new dreadful.

"Oy!" Horatio exclaimed, pulling Gideon's attention from what he suspected was a highly censored story on the manufacture of a new airship engine.

"What is it?" Doc asked.

"They've gone and cancelled the Dionysian Festival," Horatio complained. "The Hollywood Bole will be dark for the first time since it began in thirteen fifty-seven."

"Political complications?" Doc asked, reading over Horatio's shoulder.

"Buggering Midasian flu outbreak," Horatio said.

"I'm surprised they were able to keep the festival going this long," Gideon said.

Horatio peered around Doc's paper to see Gideon. "Why?"

"Rumor has it there's a war going on?"

"There's been a sodding war going on . . . and off, and on again . . . for smogging decades," Horatio reminded Gideon.

"And Hollywood's neutrality is famed for a reason," Doc added. "Besides which, I believe there's something to be said for Colonial and Coalition citizens being able to come together in peace to share ideas, art, scientific theories—"

"Military secrets," Gideon tossed in.

"Do you reckon?" Horatio looked from the paper to Gideon, and back to the paper.

"I'd bet my ration of blueberries on it," Gideon replied.

"Is that personal experience talking?" Doc asked.

"I've never been to Hollywood," Gideon said and, after an uncomfortable pause, returned to his section of the paper and, though he forced himself to finish the article he'd been reading before Horatio's outburst, his heart wasn't really in it.

Once he'd finished a political piece describing the strengths and weaknesses of the citizens running for district minister, he moved on to an op-ed decrying the rapid expansion of a crystal-based power grid in Nike, a city that already had ample energy sources from a hybrid system of bio, wind, and hydro-power.

The addition of a crystal-powered network was, according to the author, merely another example of Tenjin Corporation's continuing crusade to enrich itself at the expense of honest utility workers, as well as exemplifying the very values that had led to Earth's destruction.

As one familiar with selfish behaviors that had a negative impact on others, Gideon could sympathize, but the author of the piece had to be pretty swarming naive if they believed a few impassioned paragraphs would have an impact on the citizenry, much less strike a chord with the district ministers whose pockets were probably lined by Tenjin Corporation "donations."

He turned from the politics of the day with some relief, flipping the page to the bottom half of the fold, and was immediately struck by the headline: *Nikean Native Awarded Posthumous Medal of Honor*.

Something in his belly clutched at the title, but he continued to read the article in silence, while at his side Doc and Horatio quibbled over a piece from Doc's section proposing the relative merits of another expedition into the Amazon Mountain Range.

He read the article through once, each word of the dry report burning into his brain. Then he read it again, hoping—as a child reading a poorly graded report might hope—that the words had rearranged themselves into a different story.

A story that didn't mock the choice he'd made, four years ago.

When, on the second study, the article remained unchanged, Gideon folded the paper with care, and with care rose from the bench. The air was cooling, he noted, but nowhere near as cold as the chill resting in his chest.

Doc asked if he was all right, and Gideon must have given a sensible response, because there were no further questions, and Gideon made his silent way out of the yard, into the cell block and up the rattling allusteel stairs to his floor without speaking to another soul.

Entering his cell, he stretched out on the thin cot and, for once, did not turn to read the names of the six soldiers killed at Nasa before closing his eyes and waiting, in that very private darkness, for the official lights out.

When morning came, Gideon rose and performed his morning exercises, just as always.

He went to the mess, and sat at the same table, with the same companions, listened to the morning grousing, mixed in with any fresh gossip, and responded when a response was required.

When the meal ended, he joined the other members of his work party in the passenger crawler. He ignored the ruts and bumps of the journey, and on arrival at the site, headed to his assigned section, tools in hand.

But on reaching his station, a sparkling spit of buzzing crystal he shared with Pavel and Horatio, he remained standing, staring out at the desert.

"You planning on meditating the crystal out of the ground?" Pavel asked.

At the question, Gideon turned to face Pavel, the violent offender who would likely never be able to function outside of the rigors of the Barrens.

"Gideon?" Horatio also straightened. "You all right then?"

Rather than respond, Gideon let his gaze trail down the vein, and the dozen or so convicts working it. Pirates, thieves, and murderers—all digging into the hard-packed earth to free the hunks of crystal-rich shard for the benefit of a world that had happily forgotten they existed.

"Gideon?" This time it was Pavel trying to get his attention.

He looked up at the giant, and for once, Pavel had no trouble reading his expression.

"Are you sure?" Pavel asked, his voice unwontedly gentle.

"Sure?" Horatio echoed, stepping away from his work. "Sure about what?"

By this time, the cessation of activity around Gideon had spread down the line to Lonnie, and then Joss, and Mama.

"What's going on here?" CO Tullaine wandered up to where Gideon stood, still looking at Pavel. "Someone find a scorpion nest?"

"No," Gideon replied before anyone else could. Then he turned to Pavel and said, "Yes."

Then the big man's brow furrowed in what, Gideon realized with a distant sort of surprise, was sadness.

"I'm sorry," he said to Pavel. Then, before anyone else could burden him with their care, turned from the party and began to walk away.

"Quinn!" Tullaine called.

"Gideon?" Horatio added, sounding a bit desperate. "What are you doing? Smog it, where's he going?"

Gideon continued on, not looking back as Pavel tried to explain, or when Tullaine, and Woo and Finch, as well, ordered the remaining inmates back to work.

He was impressed that the hubbub didn't even start to ease off until he reached step number forty-seven.

At least the dregs of Fortune would miss him.

For a time.

CHAPTER 28
DAY 1561

"I don't get it," Renny said as Gideon finished the tale.

"Don't get what?"

"Why you're here."

Gideon stared at the other man. "I just told you."

"No, you didn't."

"Yes, I did."

"You said you read an article in a newspaper."

"Yes." Gideon nodded.

"About a dead soldier."

"Yes."

"You never said who died!"

"Oh." Gideon thought back, realized Renny had the right of it. "It was Hamish."

"Who, again?"

"Hamish Costanza . . . one of my officers." He angled his head in Renny's direction. "You might remember him from the night we stole the *Bounty*? He sang that really annoying song you used to whistle—*oh*," he said, blinking as it struck. "Is that why you were whistling it all the time?"

"I can't believe it took you this long to put that together," Renny said, his voice arid as the ground on which they sat.

Gideon couldn't either, but then, he'd never liked the song.

"So Hamish was a member of your company?" Renny asked.

"One of the six who survived Nasa," Gideon confirmed.

"And now he's dead?"

"Cut down by a Midasian sword near the Asgard border. He was covering the retreat of his fellow sappers," Gideon said. "They made it. He didn't."

For a moment all was quiet, but for a quick rustle of motion from the other side of the boulder.

"So?" Renny asked.

Gideon glanced his way. "So what?"

"So, one of your old company died in battle. It's a war. It happens. Why would his death send you off in search of your own?"

"Because he's the reason I'm here!" Gideon's throat was too abused to manage a shout, but it was enough to elicit a hiss from somewhere behind his boulder.

Renny thought about that. "I thought you were here because you committed treason."

"I *confessed* to committing treason," Gideon clarified. "And I confessed so Hamish and the rest of the company wouldn't be put in front of a firing squad."

"So you were all traitors?"

"None of us were traitors," Gideon told him. "I was framed by a corrupt, Earth-bound general."

"How melodramatic," Renny judged. "Why?"

"I don't know." Gideon sank back against the rock. "He said something at the end, but . . . it didn't make any sense, so I still don't know."

"And meanwhile, you took the fall to protect your under-lings. How idiotically noble."

"I suppose you'd have let them die."

"Goes without saying." Renny shrugged. "So, to sum up, you made a bad deal to protect Hamish and the rest of your motley crew. Hamish then smogged the deal by dying to save his new company—obviously bad decisions roll downhill—and because of that, you've decided to chuck it all and die a slow, horrible, meaningless death."

"Better than living a long, sunsburned, pointless life," Gideon said bitterly. "Isn't that why you left?"

"Yes, but I'm me, and you're you."

"What is that supposed to mean?"

"It means all I had was hate, while you are the living, breathing—for now, at any rate—epitome of Johnny on the Spot."

"Who?"

"You know," Renny chided. "The Old Earth term for a person who's always there when trouble is brewing, but more, the one who will step between that trouble and whoever it's meant for."

"And why would Johnny do that?"

"Possibly because he lives with the delusion that his actions make a difference?"

"Johnny sounds like an idiot," Gideon decided.

"Truer words."

Gideon replied with a sneer.

"And now I'm expected to believe that you, unlike poor Johnny, are no longer living under the same delusion?"

"Believe what you want," Gideon said. "Because now that I've done what you asked . . . and asked, and *asked* . . . and told you why I'm out here, I'll be moving along now. Alone."

And the sooner the better, as the suns had sunk far enough

that Tyche was halfway below the horizon. Soon, Nemesis would follow, and hard on their heels would come the moons, and the cold of the night.

Perfect weather for a body wanting to put as much distance between himself and salvation as possible.

With that intent, he put a hand down to shove himself to his feet—and immediately snatched it back with a curse.

"What is it?" Renny leaned over the skeleton.

"You're still here?"

"Obviously. Is it a scorpion?" Renny asked. "An adder? Ooh, maybe it's a tarantula."

"It's not a tarantula, it's a cut." Gideon held up his hand to show the dark red line welling along the calloused palm.

"A ghost can dream," Renny sighed.

"We don't believe in ghosts," Gideon reminded him, his gaze dipping to the ground where he spied, not the jagged edge of bone or rock that he'd expected, but a slender, oily seam of black peeking through the sand next to the tooth-marked tibia.

"What is it?" Renny asked.

Rather than answer, Gideon carefully brushed the drifted sand away to reveal a gleaming—and all too familiar—length of shard.

"Huh," Renny said. "So that's where that went."

"This is . . . you?" Gideon asked, staring at the skeleton.

"Apparently?" Renny said, pursing his lips as he studied the pathetic remains.

"How can you not know?" Gideon asked, peering at the pale figure.

"I've never seen me from this particular view," Renny pointed out dryly, then grimaced. "I don't seem to have aged well. Careful with that," he added as Gideon drew the warm length of shard from its burial ground.

Gideon raised the slick black dagger, mindful of the edge, as the rags Renny had used for a grip disintegrated at his touch. He watched them fall, shreds and patches of bleached gray, drifting like ash to the desert floor.

He looked at Renny. "Did you use it?"

"Why?" Renny asked back. "Do you want to quit? Ah, but I forget," Renny continued before Gideon could find a response. "You already have. It's just a matter of your body catching up with the idea. And it will, eventually," he promised as Gideon held up the shard, now gleaming wetly in the light of the setting Nemesis. "But until it does, there's a long, cold, thirsty night to get through, followed by another long, sunburned, thirsty day before you'll be allowed to leave the field of battle."

"But you stopped here," Gideon said.

"Perhaps I did," Renny said. "But I was always one for taking the easy way out, wasn't I?" He straightened from his crouch and stared down while Gideon continued to look at the inky dagger. "Is that what you want?" he asked. "To take the easy way?"

Gideon continued to stare at the shard, thinking of that night ahead, and the day after, then frowned as the rustles he'd heard earlier resolved into a spatter of earth, and a familiar hissing.

"Well?" Renny asked as Gideon rolled to his knees to look around. "What are you waiting for?"

"Quiet," Gideon ordered, tilting his head to listen.

"Rude," Renny commented, but sprang back when Gideon forced himself to his feet. "Wait." He waved his hands as Gideon started to walk away from the pile of bones. "Where are you going?"

"I want to see what's making that noise."

"What noise?" Renny, predictably, followed Gideon around the pile of rocks that had sheltered his remains, and halted, as Gideon did, on spying the source of the wind-like whispers.

Here, in a hollowed-out nest, amidst the ruin of what had been a clutch of eggs, a single draco hatchling was crouched. Wings not-yet-dry flapped at the ghostly shape of the viper that Gideon guessed was responsible for the destruction of the rest of the eggs.

Gideon felt a small tickle under his heart at the sight of the tiny draconette—it was, at best, half the size of his own hand—flapping and snapping at the viper's weaving head.

Even as he internally cheered for the little guy, the viper hissed and recoiled, its hood flaring.

Gideon's hand tightened around the shard.

"You have got to be joking," Renny's hiss echoed the viper's. "You're not really thinking of getting in the middle of this?"

"Shut up, Renny," Gideon said, moving around the rocks.

"Fine." Renny's voice was a shrug. "Leap into the fray like always. But, and also like always, your actions won't make any difference."

"Why not?" Gideon asked, despite himself.

"A new-hatched draconette won't last the night without its mother," Renny said, pointing to a motionless hump that, when Gideon looked closer, proved to be the body of a fully grown draco.

Gideon felt a twist in his chest as Renny's truth landed.

Sure, he could save the fledgling life now, but only in favor of a longer, slower, death.

Not much of a victory.

But even as he began to turn away, the viper uncoiled and sprang forward, only to strike a bit of shell, because the draconette had also jumped, just high enough to avoid becoming viper chow, while emitting a high-pitched keen that Gideon thought was meant to be intimidating.

As the tiny reptile flapped its wings in an approximation of a landing, Gideon let out a guttural, "*Smog it.*"

"You'll only live to regret it," Renny promised.

"You had your chance," Gideon snarled, before leaping in to join the fight.

CHAPTER 29
DAY 1561 - 1562

EXHAUSTION, THIRST, AND HEATSTROKE MADE FOR A sketchy leap, and a worse landing, but even while he landed hard on one knee, Gideon drove the shard deep into the viper's bloated, immobile middle.

That's what you get for gorging, Gideon thought as the snake lashed wildly on either side of the weapon.

At his left, the draconette hop-fluttered closer, hissing its own anger at the viper.

"You tell him," Gideon said, falling back on his heels.

"Mind the snake," Renny said.

"Wha—*Ow!*" Gideon flicked his right hand, but the viper, not yet aware of its demise, hung on.

With a few of his drill sergeant's favorite curses, he opted to pound the remaining vestiges of life out of the stubborn reptile with a handy stone.

"That's the third viper you've killed," Renny observed. "The Keepers are going to put a warrant out."

"Go away, Renny."

"I wish I could."

When the snake finally ceased twitching, Gideon withdrew

the shard pinning it to the ground and, with a grimace, used it to slice the bite open, allowing the venom to bleed out.

At his side, the draconette fluttered and let out a worried-sounding croon.

"It's okay," Gideon told him. He glanced at the dead mama draco and considered the lack of numbness in his wounded hand. "I don't think it had too much venom left."

In response, the draconette climbed onto Gideon's leg, where it reared on its hind legs and let out a piteous cry.

"Uh-oh. I think he's hungry. Are you hungry?"

The draco's cry redoubled.

"I'll take that as a yes." Gideon paused, thought. "What do little dracos eat?"

"How would I know?" Renny asked when Gideon looked at him.

"Useful as ever," Gideon complained, and turned to the tiny creature. "So, what do you want for breakfast? Wait," he said, suddenly inspired. "How about some fresh desert viper?"

"Eww," Renny said.

"Think of it as poetic justice," Gideon told him, coaxing the fledgling into the palm of his uninjured hand and scootching over to the deceased snake. "There you go," he said, holding the baby up to the front half of the corpse.

The draconette chirped, very like a bird, and crawled from Gideon's hand to perch on the remains.

As Gideon watched, he poked at the scales with his pointed muzzle—very beak-like, now Gideon got a close look—then looked to Gideon and chirped again.

Then it cried again.

Which was when it hit Gideon how very much like a bird the dracos were, and that a mama draco probably fed her brood in the same way a mama bird did.

"Oh, boy," he muttered, his gorge rising even as he reclaimed the shard he'd let fall while cleaning out the bite.

"Never have I ever been so happy to be dead," Renny said as Gideon made the first cut.

Gideon said nothing—mostly because if he spoke he might start dry heaving—and did the needful.

He tried, and almost succeeded, to convince himself it wasn't too different from the time he and Dani had gone to a restaurant in the Ford city of Epsilon that featured a series of uncooked dishes.

He even, once the draco had inhaled the offerings Gideon provided, forced himself to swallow a few bites of the inadvertent dinner himself.

"Well, now you've done it," Renny said as the draco crawled back onto Gideon's leg.

"Done what?" Gideon stroked a gentle finger down the scaled back, noting the warmth. Not like a reptile at all.

"Saved yet another small, unregarded life. Worse, you've committed to keeping it alive."

Gideon's eyes rose to find Renny lounging on the other side of the viper's remains. By now the suns were truly set and Renny, like the rest of the desert, had become a pale rendition of himself.

"I guess I have," Gideon admitted, looking down at the tiny beast, watching the first of its lids dip.

"But will it be enough?" Renny asked.

Gideon looked up. "What do you mean?"

"You know what I mean . . . Colonel Gideon Quinn, commander of the Dirty Dozen. The man who stole the *Bounty*, and the Midasian cannon blueprints. You're the soldier who convinced a Coalition Mech Brigade to attack their own allies! What sort of satisfaction can you hope to find in a lifetime spent stepping between vipers and dracos, villainous guards and inmates, villainous inmates and guards, Pavel and . . . everyone?"

"That's not what it's about," Gideon said, surprising himself with the sudden realization. "That's never what it was about."

"Let's suppose I believe that," Renny said after a beat. "What happens when there's another Hamish? Or another Cassandra? Because there will always be another loss."

Gideon remained silent for a moment, then glanced down at the sleeping draco. "I guess I'll just have to make sure there are more wins."

"And there's that ridiculous optimism I always despised."

Gideon's lips quirked. Then he turned to the east where the moons were rising, washing the desert in waves of silver and telling him he had a good twelve to thirteen hours of night left.

He could probably make it in nine.

"As fun as this has been, it's time for me to go," he said aloud.

When he heard no answer, he looked up, then all around, but nowhere did he see a hint of snarky hallucination.

"Okay?" he said, frowning at the empty space, then looked at the curled-up draco, its tail twitching lightly near its nose. "Okay," he said again. "I guess it's just you and me."

By the time the moons were well risen, Gideon, dangling a viper tail in one hand, was retracing his steps toward Morton.

The little guy had woken from his nap, and now perched on Gideon's shoulder, one taloned paw resting behind his ear.

The moons had climbed high enough that, if Gideon looked back, he might have seen their light reflecting from the shard Gideon had planted atop the mound of sand he'd piled over Renny's bones.

But he didn't look back.

Back, he'd discovered, didn't tell the whole story.

Instead, he fixed his attention on his path, and the people waiting at the other end.

He even allowed himself to think of Dani, and how he never wanted her to learn he'd taken the long walk.

He never wanted her to think he'd taken the easy way.

"And who knows," he said aloud as tiny talons pricked through his shirt, "we could still see her again. Someday. Somehow."

The draco's tail twitched, and it trilled in what sounded like agreement.

Gideon's lips tugged in a smile. A real smile. "I guess we should come up with a name for you," he said to his scaled companion. "Any ideas?"

In response, the draconette let out a ululating croon and, possibly because he was thinking of Dani, the sound put Gideon in mind of her favorite classical artist.

"Elvis it is," he said, and continued to retrace the shadowy path he'd first taken on the long walk from despair.

Gideon Quinn returns in *Fortune's Fool,* now available. Meanwhile, turn the page for a preview of the *Errant* crew's job-gone-wrong in *Outrageous Fortune.*

PREVIEW:
OUTRAGEOUS
FORTUNE

FORTUNE CHRONICLES 2

PROLOGUE

UCAS Kodiak
Approaching Nasa Escarpment
Treicember 21, 1442 After Landing

Captain John Pitte entered the bridge of the *Kodiak* with blood on his hands and fury in his eyes. He tried to control his limp, but every step he took felt as if his knee were stabbing itself from within.

Someday, he'd have to see about getting that shrapnel removed.

"Captain on bridge!" Sergeant Millar, the duty provost, announced.

"As you were," John said, brushing past the prov, his steps thudding unevenly on the deck as he approached the command dais where General Jessup Rand had stationed himself, hands clasped behind his back and attention fixed on the Nasa Escarpment, which loomed ever larger through the forward windows.

John, crossing the deck, took a deep breath of the familiar

allusteel and oil mix, slightly tainted by the coppery odor of blood he brought with him. He felt the deck inclining slightly as the helm adjusted the *Kodiak*'s altitude.

Other than the thrum of the engines and accompanying clanks, pings, and clicks of the airship's workings, the bridge was quiet.

John was within a few steps of the dais when Rand finally turned to acknowledge his presence. Eyebrows rising, the general stepped away from the forward rail and crossed to the aft steps.

"Captain."

"General." John continued until he reached the foot of the dais.

Rand's dark face tipped down, then up. "You appear to be injured."

"Bad turn on the ladder," John said, looking up at Rand. As he did, he noticed a shadow emerging from the far side of the dais.

A shadow which resolved itself into Sergeant Jihan, General Rand's aide de camp.

"That was fast," John said to Jihan, whom he'd left on the *Kodiak*'s lowest deck not fifteen minutes past.

Jihan offered a salute but said nothing, adding to the heavy silence of the bridge, which pressed on John from all sides in a way utterly unfamiliar to him.

Possibly because it was no longer *his* bridge, not in any way that mattered, not with Rand in control of the *Kodiak* and the helm, elevator, and nav all being operated by Rand's officers.

Even Millar, the duty prov who'd called John's presence, had come aboard with the general currently studying John's uniform with obvious distaste.

Perhaps Rand objected to the sight of blood.

"You are out of uniform, Captain," Rand said, confirming John's supposition.

"And your man is out of order, General," John replied, his eyes darting to where Jihan stood at the foot of the dais. "Provost Millar," he called over his shoulder, "please place Sergeant Jihan under warrant for assault and conduct unbecoming a member of the Corps."

"Belay that, Millar," Rand called over John's shoulder. "Captain." He stepped forward but remained on the dais. "As I am certain Jihan would have told you, he was acting on my orders. It was your man, McCabe, whose behavior called for punishment."

"Punishment," John repeated.

"For dereliction of duty," Jihan inserted at the general's nod.

John didn't look at the sergeant. "Assuming I believe that, which I don't, since when did the Colonial Corps adopt the Coalition's use of the lash?"

"Since the dereliction in question endangered an entire airship," Rand countered.

"Gunner's Mate McCabe failed to report a faulty containment cell in one of his cannons," Sergeant Jihan inserted so promptly it struck John as rehearsed. "If I hadn't noticed the damage, the *Kodiak* might have been lost with all hands."

"You do get around," John murmured, sparing the general's aide a cold glance.

"My aide knows I like a full picture."

John turned back to Rand. "If such negligence occurred, it would still call for a full investigation and the convening of a court-martial, not the draco's tail in the cargo bay with no witnesses."

Rand's eyebrows rose. "I'd suggest you calm yourself, Captain Pitte."

"I believe myself to be quite calm," John said, briefly taken aback. He'd not raised his voice once, except to get Millar's attention.

"In that case you might, in your cool-headedness, recall that a commander has the right to enact field justice in a time of war."

"And as I am McCabe's commander, it was my right to make that determination," John reminded the general . . . calmly. "Yet somehow neither these accusations nor this—field justice—came to my attention. Had my first officer not come across McCabe being dragged below decks, I'd still not have known."

Even as he said this, John saw something flash in the general's expression, something like satisfaction.

"And I remind *you*," Rand said, "that for the duration of this mission, a mission that involves recovering an entire company of deserters, the *Kodiak* and her crew are mine to command."

"With respect," John said, "in all matters *not* relating to your mission, such as the day-to-day running of the *Kodiak*, the 'ship and crew are *my* responsibility, and that includes all matters of crew performance."

And there John spied it, again, that flash of satisfaction in the other man's expression.

"It pains me to admit, but you may be correct, Captain Pitte," Rand said, glancing at Jihan, who nodded and stepped from his position to stand behind John. "Mr. McCabe is of your crew, which makes him your responsibility and *your* failure. As such, I am compelled to order the surrender of your command—"

"Excuse me?" John stepped forward.

"—until such time as a full inquiry determines the level of your complicity in your crew's negligence," Rand continued, nodding at his aide.

Jihan reached for John's sword, but John snatched the sergeant's wrist. "No," he said quietly.

"Don't make this difficult, sir," Jihan said.

"Captain," Moncivais called from the radio alcove, "I'm receiving word of groundside movement from the crow's nest."

John shoved Jihan away. "What kind—"

"What kind of movement?" Rand cut in. "Where on the ground?"

Moncivais looked at John, who gave a short nod, and turned to Rand. "Sir, crow's nest reports spying several individuals at the top of the Nasa Escarpment. She can't make a positive ID as the suns are setting, but they are there, and armed."

"The deserters. Just as I expected," Rand said. "Radio." He turned to Moncivais. "Contact Commander O'Bannion and tell her to have her jump teams standing by." As he spoke, he flipped the command intercom, set into the dais, to life. "This is General Rand to gunner deck. Charge all cannons and prepare to fire."

"*Cannons charging, aye,*" a tinny voice emerged from the speaker.

"Belay those orders," John called, earning a scathing glance from Millar and a confused "Sir?" from Moncivais.

"*Say again?*" came from the dais speaker.

"Did I hear you correctly, *Captain?*" Rand looked over his shoulder. "Do as you were ordered," he said to both the speaker and Moncivais before focusing on John. "You are treading on dangerous ground, Captain Pitte."

"Perhaps. But it strikes me odd that a company of alleged deserters would be standing in clear view of one their own airships."

"We're being hailed," Moncivais announced.

John, Rand, and even Sergeant Jihan turned to the radio operator.

"Put it on speaker," John ordered, ignoring Rand's hiss as Moncivais flicked the speakers to life.

"*—hailing UCAS* Kodiak *under Captain Pitte, this is Corpsman Carver, 12th Company, 96th Infantry, please respond . . .*"

"It's them," Rand said, his satisfaction palpable. "We have him."

"We have a contact," John corrected. "Request the colonel's ident for verification," he said to Moncivais. "And to specify the nature of his mission."

"Jihan," Rand said.

Just that—just *Jihan*—and before John could blink he felt it, the cold intrusion of steel into flesh. He looked down to see the point of Jihan's sword emerging above his right hip.

"Consider yourself relieved of duty," Jihan murmured in his ear, then yanked the sword out.

The force of the weapon's removal caused John to jerk back, which caused his head to bounce up, so he caught sight of Moncivais, already half risen from her chair. He had enough strength to shake his head at her—*no point.*

"*Repeat, UCAS* Kodiak *this is Corpsman Carver, 12th Company, do you read? Over.*"

John shook his head again as he heard Rand delivering targeting orders to the cannon.

"Captain John Pitte," the Jihan intoned formally, "you are hereby placed under warrant . . ."

"All cannons take aim," Rand said.

"*Repeat, repeat, Captain Pitte . . .*" the young voice continued to call over the speakers.

"*Cannons taking aim, aye.*"

"You can't," John said.

Rand didn't even spare him a glance. "I already have," he said as another voice crackled over the speaker.

"*Hey, Kodiak, this is Colonel Gideon Quinn, 12th Company. Do you read? Over.*"

"Prepare to fire on my mark," Rand snapped into the radio as he stared through the windows at the escarpment.

"*Repeat, repeat, Captain Pitte . . .*"

I'm here, John said—or rather, thought he said.

"Mark," Rand said.

Don't, John thought, even as the whine of the plasma cannons filled the air.

John looked down at the thrumming deck, noting as he did the dark red drops vibrating as they fell, and then he too was falling. And then he was on the deck, the cold metal against his cheek contrasting with the warm blood seeping from his uniform.

Lying there, unable to move or speak, he heard Carver's voice again hailing him and then, last of all . . .

"All cannons, fire at will." Rand's voice, dark with triumph, followed John into the sanguine fog.

I

Dyar's Canyon
Eastern Allianza Territories
United Colonies of Fortune
February 9, 1449 After Landing

JOHN DUCKED A SIZZLING BOLT OF PLASMA, STRAIGHTENED, and glanced at the smoking hole left in the multihued strata for which Dyar's Canyon was renowned.

Admittedly, Dyar's Canyon was also renowned for its inhospitable fauna, alkali lakes, and treacherous electrical storms, but John felt a perverse fondness for the place. It was dangerous and beautiful and defiant and didn't give a lick for the humans who'd created it.

"What the fecking comb are you waiting for?" Jagati O'Bannion, John's first mate, asked as she ran past.

"Sorry," he said, racing after her, "but these people have no respect for nature."

"Report it to the keepers," she called over her shoulder as a series of shouts, followed by more plasma bursts, had both laying a quick burst of suppressive fire before slipping single file through the jagged fissure.

"Come on, come on, come on!" Jagati hissed as she clambered over a tumble of fallen stone.

"I'm come onning," John replied, one hand on the satchel he wore crosswise over his jacket.

He'd almost reached the top of the rock pile when another shot had him diving the rest of the way over, resulting in an awkward rolling-falling-bruising affair. He continued to roll to his feet with a fresh spate of twinges. "It's entirely possible," he panted, "that taking this job was a mistake."

From the steady stream of epithets drifting back his way, he could only assume Jagati shared his opinion.

"—ing, smog-eating, spawn of a hornet," she finished as he came even with her.

A sideways glance showed the raw umber of her skin matted with the same violet grime which coated their clothes and dusted the spiraling mass of her brown-black curls. Combined with her fierce expression, the end result was rather demonic.

At least she looked threatening.

If the back of his hand was any indication, John figured he came off like a victim of some unnamed, wasting disease.

"We're close to the LZ, right?" she asked, slowing as the canyon they traversed narrowed to the width of an airship's crawlspace.

"Almost certainly," he agreed, nudging her onward while he removed the satchel and held it at his side so he could fit through the cramped fissure.

"Almost?" Stuck sideways with her head turned forward, he could only imagine her glare. "*Pitte.*"

"Best keep moving," he prompted.

She hissed but kept moving, and in a few minutes which

passed like only a few years, they squeezed through to the other side, where Jagati came to a halt and scanned the wider space.

"Pitte," she said again, which in Jagati shorthand meant *Tell me we're not lost. And if you can't tell me we're not lost, at least tell me we have a plan to become unlost. And if we don't have a plan to become unlost, feel free to present your ass for me to kick all the way back to the shadow traders' camp.*

Jagati's shorthand was an incredible time saver.

"We're not lost," he told her.

"Good."

"Except I think we should already have passed the column that looks like a mammoth's—"

"*Pitte!*"

"Oh, there it is." He pointed to the right, where the cold blaze of the noontime suns had flattened the distinctive geographic feature.

"Overcompensation," Jagati muttered, even as a rapid series of plasma bursts cut the suggestive formation down to size.

She ducked, glanced back, and cursed anew as a shadow trader emerged from the crevice.

"Almost there," John assured, ignoring the smoke curling up from a fresh plasma score on his right thigh.

"Can't be soon enough." She jogged past him, then paused. "Smog it, Pitte, you're—"

"Heads!" he warned.

She ducked, spun, and fired on the foremost outlaw. When the distant shape let out a short squeal and dropped, she backed up and tucked herself under John's shoulder.

Thus linked, they turned and ran for it while John fired off an occasional shot at their pursuers.

"That's the last tunnel." He jerked his chin forward, toward an inverted V of a passage which connected to the canyon where they'd left their airship moored.

An airship their crewmates should have fired up and ready to fly the second John and Jagati hit the gangplank.

She nodded and urged him faster. "This is more resistance than I expected. Do we even know what it is we're retrieving?"

"The client chose not to disclose that information." He disengaged his arm from her shoulder and limped into the tunnel. "When I asked, she said it was sensitive and started to cry."

"I hate when they cry," she said as she followed him into the passage. "Wait! I mean, don't wait, but . . . the client's a *she?*"

"Of course. Didn't I say?"

"Nooo . . ."

"Ah. Well, then, yes—the client is a woman," he said. "Typical spoiled risto with more money than sense. I've no doubt we're risking life and limb for her great-grandmother's 7-Up reliquary."

"Could be worse," Jagati said. "Could be another one of those ancient torture devices."

"That was a shoe. An original Louboutin, as I recall."

"You say shoe, I say spiky pain-delivery device."

"At any rate," he said, "whatever is in this satchel meant enough for the client to offer treble the usual fee for a recovery."

"It's not enough."

John didn't reply but limped faster, bracing a hand against the side of the cavern until he stepped out into the bright light of day . . . and froze in his tracks.

Behind him, Jagati came rushing out, only stopping when she ran into his back.

"What's wrong?" she asked, squeezing past him. "Shouldn't we be boarding about now?"

"It was here," he said, staring at the wide, flat, and—most importantly—empty space before them. "It was right *here.*" He peered up, shielding his eyes from the suns, and Jagati followed suit.

"Smogging toxic Earth!" Jagati stomped her foot, raising a puff of purple dust. "This! Isn't! Funny!" She ran forward into the empty place once occupied by their vessel, then she—yes—cursed some more.

"Feel better?" John asked, limping up to join her.

Her lip curled in a snarl. "What do you think?"

"Just asking," he said, giving the tunnel they'd emerged from a meaningful glance.

She growled, then gave him a punch on the shoulder, then led the way to a craggy outcropping at the base of the canyon's northern wall. "I will kill them," she muttered as she began to climb. "I will kill them and dance in their blood. I may be sorry, later, but I'll do it."

John almost smiled but knew better than to say anything.

"Here," she called down, "toss me the case."

He unslung the leather carryall and heaved it up.

Jagati caught the strap and slung the bag over the top edge of the ridge. "There's level ground up here," she called down. "And it's defensible. Sort of."

He nodded and started to climb after her, but stopped cold at a sudden rattling of stone from the canyon wall to his right. Turning, he clung to the face with one hand and shaded his eyes with the other as he searched for the sound's origin.

What he saw made him release his grip on the outcropping and drop back to the canyon floor, where his leg almost buckled under him.

"What the hell are you doing?" Jagati asked from on high.

John, in the act of raising his hands, jerked his chin upwards.

As he had, she shielded her eyes from the suns and stared in the indicated direction.

There was a telling silence from above. It told him Jagati had also spied the sniper perched at the canyon's upper edge.

Outrageous Fortune is now available.

Acknowledgments

This novella was written through some strenuous times, as the dedication may indicate, and though there was a lot of solitary effort, no book makes it to the readers without a team so let's give it up for Team Fallen, starting with Dr. Deborah King, who really did help me keep it together while everything around me was falling apart.

Many thanks also to Lori Drake, author-in-arms and venting partner.

Hugs from afar to Sandy D-L and Kelley McKinnon for their feedback.

To my family, who probably thought I'd never finish this novella, and had to put up with Grumpy Mom on the rough days, I love you all.

A round of applause for editor Claudette Cruz, sensitivity reader C.K. Brown, and cover artist Youness Elh.

And of course, thanks to **everyone reading this book**; you've chosen to spend more time on Fortune, so on behalf of Gideon, Elvis, and the rest of the cast, thank you for visiting.

About the Author

As a lifelong fan of complex characters and outrageous worlds, I lean on my history in theatre, fight choreography, and parenting to create immersive adventures, engaging characters, and unlikely partnerships (because I pretty much live for oddballs teaming up against a bad system).

I can also be found hanging out at Ream Stories, growing more outrageous adventures featuring flawed heroes, chosen families, and all the snark you care to entertain.*

*__True story:__ *In first grade, my youngest turned in a daily journal entry featuring the opening phrase, "Sometimes, my mommy can be sarcastic."***

**I've never felt more seen.*

MORE OUTRAGEOUS FICTION

THE FORTUNE CHRONICLES
Soldier of Fortune
Fortune's Fallen
Outrageous Fortune
Change of Fortune
Fortune's Fool
THE ZODIAC FILES
The Gemini Hustle
The Libra Gambit